"We need to go, Caroline. *Now*."

Zane shoved her ahead of him. The headlights bearing down on them grew even brighter. The screaming of the tow truck engine grew shriller. They were just at the edge of the highway when Zane heard the crash of an impact as the heavily reinforced truck plowed into their pickup.

Something hit him behind his right knee, knocking him to the ground and sending him tumbling down an embankment. He heard other pieces of debris crashing into the trees and underbrush around him. Then the lights from the attacking truck suddenly went out and Zane was falling in darkness. Finally, he came to a stop.

"Caroline?" he called out, heart thundering in his chest and sick with fear that she'd been hurt.

She didn't answer.

He got to his feet, relieved to find that his knee wasn't badly injured, and called her name again. And again, he didn't hear her respond.

Zane frantically looked around. Caroline had been beside him just a minute ago. Now she was gone...

Jenna Night comes from a family of Southern-born natural storytellers. Her parents were avid readers and the house was always filled with books. No wonder she grew up wanting to tell her own stories. She's lived on both coasts, but currently resides in the inland northwest, where she's astonished by the occasional glimpse of a moose, a herd of elk or a soaring eagle.

Books by Jenna Night

Love Inspired Suspense

Last Stand Ranch
High Desert Hideaway
Killer Country Reunion

KILLER COUNTRY REUNION

JENNA NIGHT

HARLEQUIN® LOVE INSPIRED® SUSPENSE

Recycling programs
for this product may
not exist in your area.

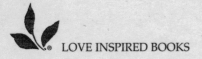

LOVE INSPIRED BOOKS

ISBN-13: 978-1-335-54384-4

Killer Country Reunion

www.Harlequin.com

Printed in U.S.A.

The Lord is my rock, and my fortress, and my deliverer;
my God, my strength, in whom I will trust...
–Psalms 18:2

To my mother, Esther. I'm remembering the cry of the whip-poor-will in the Blue Ridge Mountains of Virginia.

Acknowledgments

Many thanks to Elizabeth Mazer, a Killer Editor.

ONE

Caroline Marsh wiped the tears from her cheeks with the back of her hand and sat down on a bench outside, taking a moment to compose herself.

She turned her gaze to the waters of nearby Lake Cobalt, trying to decide whether it would be wiser to let herself have a good hard cry and get it all out of her system, or choke back her grief again—something she'd done a lot, lately.

The attorney she'd just met with had handed over a stack of paperwork and confirmed that, as of today, Caroline was officially the legal owner of her late brother's business. It was still hard to talk about Owen in the past tense. To acknowledge that her younger brother was really, *really* gone. His body had been found floating in Seattle's Elliot Bay, 350 miles to the west, with evidence of blunt force trauma to the back of his head. In the aftermath there'd been no arrests. No suspects identified. Nothing but an open police case that seemed to be going nowhere.

She clutched the sheaf of papers, held together with a black binder clip, a little tighter. Despite the digital age, some things still required paper and actual ink signatures. So here it was, printed in black and white—the official, legal proof that her brother had left her his business and his house so that she'd be equipped to take care of the most precious thing in his life: his son, Dylan.

Pull yourself together.

A four-year-old boy waited for her back at the house with Caroline's mom. The saddest part was that he wasn't just waiting for her. A couple of times Caroline had seen him walk to the front window around sundown, his ever-watchful dog, Millie, at his side, to look for Owen. The boy seemed to forget, or perhaps he still didn't understand, that his dad was never coming home. Every time the heartache over her brother, and for his son, had brought her to tears in front of the boy. She would not let that happen again.

Caroline had little experience dealing with children. She had lived in California while Dylan was growing up here in Idaho. But she was pretty certain it would be best for her nephew if she walked through the door at the house with her shoulders back and a smile on her face. Or at least the closest approximation of a smile she could muster.

A white van pulled up into the parking lot and she heard the side door slide open. It sounded like it was idling at the curb near where she was sitting.

At the same time, she realized a little late-afternoon rain was starting to sprinkle on her legal documents. The lakeside air was already pretty chilly, anyway. Time to go.

She looked up and saw a man walking toward her from the van. His black knit cap was pulled down low. The collar of his jacket was flipped up and concealed the bottom of his face. He strode purposefully, his gaze locked on her eyes.

Unease gnawed at the pit of Caroline's stomach. The man's behavior was odd. She thought of Owen and icy fear seeped into her chest. She slid the strap of her purse over her shoulder, took a quick look down at the bench to make sure she wasn't leaving anything behind and glanced up.

The man lifted his right hand, calmly pointed a gun at her face and fired.

With a burst of energy born of sheer terror, Caroline lunged down and threw the right side of her body across the bench. At the same time she felt a burning sensation rip across the top of her left shoulder.

Dear God, what's happening?

The gunman continued walking forward, pointing his gun down toward her head, which she now pressed against the seat of the bench. There was a silencer on the end of the gun barrel. Her father had been a cop. She knew what a silencer looked like. If no one heard the shots, no one would come to her rescue. Not until it was too late.

Do something.

She grabbed the bundle of papers that had slid onto the bench and flung it at him. The binder clip collided with the bridge of his nose and his head snapped back.

Heart pounding in her chest, Caroline shoved herself up off the bench and started running.

The van was still idling at the parking lot curb, so she ran in the opposite direction, toward the lake.

The office complex had two levels. The bottom level was a wooden boardwalk built along the edge of Lake Cobalt. It was Friday afternoon and most people had already cleared out for the weekend. Right now, there was nobody else in sight.

Caroline sprinted for the stairs leading down to the offices that jutted out over the water. Grabbing the newel post, she flung herself around the end of the banister and down, taking the steps two at a time, moving as fast as she could go. She tried to yell for help as she ran, but the terror flooding her body gripped her lungs so tightly that it was all she could do to keep breathing.

She reached the bottom step and a bullet flew past her, tearing up the wooden planking by her right foot.

She ran harder, veering to her left around a corner where she caught her foot on the leg of a bistro table, part of one of the many wrought iron sets placed around the boardwalk. Unable to catch her balance, she fell on her face, stunning herself for the first few seconds. Scrambling to right herself, she saw a smoked-glass office door straight ahead with a light glowing inside the office. She ran for it, grabbed the handle and pulled. It didn't budge.

"Help!" Desperate, Caroline pounded on the door with one hand while continuing to yank on the handle with the other.

Was there even anybody in there? Terror and frustration burned through her blood like fire. She raised both fists, feeling a sharp pain in her left shoulder, and pounded on the glass door as hard as she could. "*Help!* Someone's trying to kill me! Let me in! *Please!*"

In the door's reflection she saw the gunman round the corner and jog up behind her, grinning and raising his gun.

A couple of people somewhere in the maze-like complex started yelling, but they sounded too far away to help her in time.

It ain't over till it's over. It was one of her dad's favorite expressions. He had a lot of them, and she could almost hear him in her head. *Don't you ever quit.*

She whirled around.

Do whatever it takes.

Options. What were her options? She could run, but continuing down the boardwalk along the straight, long stretch ahead would make her an easy target if the gunman knew what he was doing. She could jump into the water if she had to, but she'd never been a fast swimmer. And Cobalt was a deep lake. Besides, the water in late September was too chilly for swimming. Cold muscles would slow her down.

But jumping into the lake was the only reasonable choice she could find—the one with the best shot at keeping her alive. Too bad she'd taken so long to decide. The gunman was now just a couple of steps away from her. It was too late.

Never give up.

She frantically looked around, and then jammed her hand into a big urn-shaped planter beside the office door. She grabbed a handful of dirt and decorative rocks and threw it in the guy's face, hoping it would be enough of a distraction for her to get away.

It didn't faze him.

Ignoring the small projectiles, he snatched her arm before she could get away. "Stop fighting. It's over." He lifted his gun and pointed it at her forehead.

Someone in the office behind the locked door screamed.

Her attacker glanced in that direction. Caroline did, too, and saw three witnesses who had moved close enough to the door to be visible and were watching the struggle playing out in front of them.

Maybe in his reflection on the glass the gunman saw what Caroline had just noticed. In the chase, his collar had flattened out and the bottom half of his face was now uncovered. His beanie had also ridden up a little. His appearance was not as well hidden as it had been when he'd started. And even if she was killed, there were other witnesses now who had seen him.

Still clutching her arm, the gunman dragged her away from the door, down the boardwalk and around the corner, back toward the bottom of the stairs. Maybe it was a precaution in case he got caught. None of the witnesses would be able to testify that they'd actually seen him kill her.

Sirens wailed in the distance.

Anger at the situation flared up alongside the fear coursing through Caroline's body. She wasn't going down without a fight. She twisted her arm, trying to break his grip. When that didn't work, she kicked out her foot and tried to trip him.

Dear Lord, she prayed, forcing her thoughts away from anticipating the shot that would end this battle. *Please protect Dylan.*

Who would take care of him if she was gone? Caroline's mom experienced lingering damage from a heart attack that made her tire more easily than she used to. She could look after the boy for several hours a day now while he was still small, freeing Caroline to take care of all the necessary legal matters, but it wasn't a permanent solution. The task of raising him as he grew older would likely be too much for her mother, meaning she wouldn't be able to take custody.

Dylan's biological mother, Michelle, had decided after eight months of motherhood that she was wasting her youth and missing out on too much fun. She'd walked out on Owen and Dylan, severed all ties and filed for divorce. Through friends in town who'd seen her, Owen knew she'd fallen in with an unsavory crowd. He'd told Caroline that while his ex-wife had never been convicted of a crime, her boyfriend had been locked up on several occasions for a variety of offenses. Most involved drugs.

Owen had mentioned to Caroline that he suspected his former wife used drugs. For that reason, and because he realized their mother's health was fragile, he had requested in his will that Caroline be given custodianship of Dylan should something happen to him. The court system had agreed.

The poor kid no longer had his dad. And he hadn't seen his mom or anyone in her family since he was an infant. He had his grandma, but he needed Caroline, too. She couldn't die—not here, not today. Not when that precious boy needed her.

"No!" Exhausted from running and fighting, Caroline somehow summoned up the

surge of strength she needed to twist her body away from the gunman and finally break free of his grip.

Then something happened. She couldn't see what it was because the action was behind her. But suddenly the full weight of the gunman—plus more—was pressing on her and she was knocked down to the boardwalk. She smacked her head and saw a few sparkles of light. A feeling of drowsiness threatened to overtake her but she fought against it. If she allowed her heavy eyelids to drop shut, that would be the end of everything.

Zane Coleman kept his focus on the man's gun. Two tours in Afghanistan had trained him well, guaranteeing he'd never lose sight of a bad guy's weapon.

Hearing a woman scream "No!" he'd dropped the ranch expansion permits he'd just picked up at the Jefferson County building department and raced to the stairs. He'd run down the first four or five steps before taking a flying leap and tackling a man who was grabbing a woman and holding a gun. His hard landing knocked the wind out of him, but he could tell it did the same to the bad guy, too.

The woman, also knocked down when Zane

landed on the guy, was likely getting her face pushed into the boardwalk. But there wasn't anything he could do about that right now. His focus was on shoving his left hand onto the back of the man's left shoulder to keep him pinned in place while he reached with his right hand to yank the handgun from the man's grip.

Unfortunately, the gunman recovered faster than Zane anticipated. Still gripping his gun tightly, the man squirmed and shifted until he'd made enough room to bend his right arm. Zane wanted to punch him and knock him out, but he didn't dare release his grip on the guy's shoulder or his gun hand. With just a couple inches of room for movement, the jerk could easily kill the woman he'd attacked. Or he could shift the angle of the gun a little and shoot Zane instead.

Struggling to hold the bigger, heavier guy down, Zane managed to draw in a deep breath of air. Slightly more energized, he pressed harder on the guy's left shoulder and grunted as he tightened his right hand, determined to wrestle the gun from the man's grip. This time his fingers touched metal and then he felt the textured surface of the gun's handle beneath the heel of his hand. He just about had it.

The guy jerked his arm and flung the gun.

It slid until coming to a rest precariously balanced on the edge of the boardwalk, with part of the barrel hovering over the water.

The deep boom of a shotgun blast blew past him, followed by the sound of buckshot ripping through the boardwalk beside Zane and the gunman.

"Get up!" The guy with the shotgun commanded. He ratcheted another cartridge into the shotgun's chamber.

Zane heard the woman crying. She was also praying. He couldn't make out every word, but it sounded as if she was praying for someone other than herself.

Emergency sirens wailed from a couple of blocks away. Then they went silent. Which meant they were probably cop cars and they'd just rolled into the parking lot.

"I said, *get up!*"

Cautiously, Zane got to his feet. His thoughts were racing. He might not be able to prevent himself from getting shot, but he could probably do something to keep the woman alive and make sure these guys got caught.

"Hurry up!" shotgun guy barked. "Turn around and let me see your hands."

Zane complied.

Shotgun guy was short and stocky. He wore a baseball cap and dark glasses. He'd come halfway down the stairway and stopped. Now he continued down the stairs and took a couple of steps closer to Zane.

Behind him, Zane heard the first gunman get to his feet.

Zane slowly took a step back, then turned his head slightly so he could see what the original attacker was doing.

"Take care of her and let's go." Shotgun guy said to his accomplice, still keeping his weapon pointed at Zane.

Zane figured once they killed the woman they'd kill him, too. They weren't going to leave a witness behind.

The woman had stopped crying. From the corner of his eye he could see her getting to her feet, but he didn't dare turn his head far enough to get a good look at her. Not with that shotgun trained on him.

The boardwalk planks behind Zane squeaked with the sound of sudden movement. The original gunman swore, and Zane glanced over his shoulder to see the woman scrambling to get the handgun where it lay on the edge of the boardwalk.

The gunman shoved her aside and frantically reached for it, knocking it off the boardwalk. He immediately dropped down so he was lying on his belly and lunged his upper body into the lake. He brought the handgun out, its barrel dripping water. Cursing again, he rolled to his side, rose up on his elbow, pointed the gun at the woman, who appeared to be searching for something to hide behind, and fired.

Zane's heart jumped up into his throat. Then his mind registered the dull snapping sound of the weapon. The wet gun had misfired.

Zane's feeling of relief was short-lived. Now his attention was back on shotgun guy. Thus far, he had held off on firing—probably to keep from shooting his partner. Now that the partner was a few feet away and he had a clear shot at Zane, he had no reason to hesitate. Zane quickly looked around for something he could use to defend himself.

One of the table-and-chair sets that were scattered around the boardwalk was within reach. He grabbed the back of a bistro chair with one hand while using the other hand to knock aside the shotgun barrel that was pointed at him. The shotgun broke loose from the man's grip and clattered a couple of feet across the boardwalk.

Zane whirled around and swung the heavy bistro chair. He managed to hit the first gunman who was just now getting to his feet. The blow knocked him flat on his back.

Where was the woman? Zane figured he had only a few seconds before shotgun guy recovered his weapon and started shooting.

A quick glance showed him the woman was moving toward the edge of the boardwalk, trying to get as far away from danger as she could. "Jump!" he yelled, backing toward her.

He didn't hear a splash. Why was she hesitating?

"There's no other option," he snapped. "Get in the water. *Now!*"

Seconds later he heard her hit the water.

Time was running out.

He spun and flung the bistro chair at shotgun guy who'd just recovered his weapon.

Then Zane turned and ran.

He reached the edge of the boardwalk and leapt off, the boom of a shotgun blast ringing in his ears as he hit the surface of the lake.

The frigid water was shocking as he plunged downward. He opened his eyes underwater, where everything looked dark blue and blurry. Then he kicked his feet and started upward, back toward the light.

He broke through the surface and saw the boardwalk a few feet away. He quickly looked for the two gunmen, expecting shotgun guy to open fire on him. They were nowhere in sight. *Lord, please help the cops catch them.*

He turned and saw the woman bobbing on the surface, treading water several yards away from the boardwalk. With the water this cold, he wasn't surprised that she hadn't been able to swim any farther. He swam over to her. His muscles were already knotting up from the cold water, so the going was slow.

"Hey, are you all right?" he called out when he reached her.

The only response he heard was the sound of her teeth chattering.

Dark blonde hair was plastered over her face. She reached up to move it aside, and he found himself looking into the dark brown eyes of Caroline Marsh.

A voice called out to them from the boardwalk, but Zane didn't understand a word the man was saying. He just stared at his former fiancée while she stared back.

For the span of a couple of heartbeats it felt like no time had passed since he'd last seen her.

How long had it been?

Eight years. More than enough time for Zane to think of all the things he might say to her if they ever crossed paths again. All of them were some form of a heartfelt apology.

Now here she was and he could barely put together a sentence. Could barely even breathe.

"Are you hurt?" he managed to ask again.

"I-I'm all right, Zane," she stammered, her teeth still chattering.

She lifted her hands out of the water to tuck her hair behind her ears. "Th-thank you for rescuing me. But you don't need to stay beside me. Go ahead and swim back to the boardwalk. I can take care of myself."

Despite the horrifying events she'd just been through, she lifted her chin out of the water and managed a weak version of her signature spirited smile.

It would have hurt less if she'd shot him.

Tender memories and old regrets ripped through Zane's heart. But he didn't have time to dwell on them now. The grim reality was that two determined gunmen had just tried to kill her.

What had Caroline gotten herself into?

TWO

Zane stared at Caroline as if he expected some further, bigger reaction from her.

She wasn't about to give it to him.

He could forget about her asking why he'd left town and dropped all contact when they were engaged to be married. Where he'd been. How long he'd been back in the town of Cobalt. The answers didn't matter. After eight years of wondering, she simply didn't care anymore.

Okay, that was a lie. But *he* didn't have to know she still thought about him sometimes. Not as often as she used to when he first left. Just every now and then. And each time she'd come back to Cobalt for a visit, until she'd moved back a month ago.

She was disappointed to notice that even treading water in soaking wet street clothes, the man looked good. That was something else he didn't need to know. He was more muscular than when she'd last seen him. But he had been barely twenty years old back then. His jaw and neck were thicker now. So was his chest. She couldn't help noticing that, thanks to the long-sleeved gray cowboy shirt now clinging to it.

Even during his darkest days, when he was a young criminal going nowhere just like his dad, he'd dressed like a cowboy. His dad had been a hired hand on the horse ranch where the two of them had lived. Zane had always loved horses. He was good with them. She doubted that had changed—but then, what did she know? Back in the day, she'd thought he'd never leave her. She'd been wrong about that, so maybe she never knew him at all.

"I know you're capable of taking care of yourself," he finally said, after the apparent shock of seeing her wore off. "But I'd still like to help you."

He looked at the office complex and surrounding boardwalk, then back at her. It struck her that assuming they were safe in the lake might be a mistake. She couldn't see the shooters anymore, but that didn't mean they couldn't see her. The man with the shotgun could still fire at them. And what if the other man had a backup weapon, one that wasn't waterlogged?

"A-all right." Her legs were so cold she couldn't feel them anymore. But things could have turned out far worse.

Zane swam closer to her. Despite her best efforts to fight it, a tiny flare of warmth sparked in her heart. This was the chivalrous Zane she'd fallen so deeply in love with.

But he was also the man who'd left town when he could have stayed to fight. For himself. For the future the two of them had planned together.

"Let's go," he said.

He swam toward the boardwalk. Caroline tried to follow, but her body wouldn't cooperate. Her brain commanded her chilled arms and legs to move, but they refused to obey. Her body felt weighted down, pulling her toward the bottom of the lake.

Her chin and mouth dipped into the water and the searing panic she'd fought off while on the boardwalk overtook her again in an instant. She was going to drown. Those gunmen were going to win after all. Dylan would end up in the care of a mother who wanted him now only because he came with an inheritance.

Caroline sank farther into the lake before managing to kick her uncooperative legs enough to push her face out of the water a little bit. "N-no!" She forced all her strength into the word, but it came out as a whisper. Zane must have heard it, though. He turned around and swam back to her.

"D-Dylan," she managed to chatter when he got closer. "My mom." She'd just had a horrifying thought. What if the bad guys had gotten away and were headed to the house?

"We'll take care of them." Zane swam behind her, wrapped his left arm across the front of her shoulders and pulled her close so that her back was pressed against his muscled chest. "Right now we've got to take care of you," he said, his breath warm against her ear. "I've got you."

No, he did *not*. She wouldn't be fooled again. He did *not* have a strong hold on her, he was *not* looking out for her and he was *not* a man she could depend on. She'd trusted him for all those things before and he'd let her down.

But there was no way she could get out of this freezing cold water on her own. Right now she had to rely on him. She had no choice.

A sob caught in her throat as she again imagined her mom and Dylan in danger. With her brother gone, the responsibility to take care of what was left of the family rested on her shoulders. What if she'd already failed?

As they moved through the water Caroline caught a glimpse of flashing blue-and-red lights in the office complex parking lot. A paramedic and an emergency medical technician stood alongside a cop on the edge of the boardwalk close to the water. Each of the medical responders was stepping into a bright orange cold-water rescue suit. Seconds later, she heard a couple of splashes. She and Zane were nearly to the boardwalk now, so the medical responders quickly reached them.

When the rescuers tried to tug the two of them apart, Zane held her tightly, as if he were reluctant to let her go. She tilted her face upward to look at him. He turned toward her until his slightly beard-roughened chin pressed against her temple. She felt herself drifting back toward the memory of an old familiar feeling.

And then a cold wavelet smacked her in the face and snapped her out of it.

Zane didn't just break *her* heart. He broke the heart of everyone in her family who had also loved him.

The EMT trying to rescue Caroline pulled on her arm a little harder, said something to Zane and Zane finally let her go.

She was hoisted up onto the boardwalk, wrapped in blankets and taken to an accommodating insurance broker's office just a few feet away. The EMT explained that, after witnessing what had happened to Caroline and Zane, the owner had sent her employees home for the day and offered emergency personnel use of her office.

Caroline sat in a chair near a heating vent while the paramedic took her vital signs. Zane walked in a few seconds later and dropped down into a chair across from her. He locked eyes with her, his mouth set in a worried frown.

"Caroline, can you tell me what happened?" Sergeant Matt Barrow of the Cobalt Police Department—who'd joined the force just before Caroline's father was killed in the line of duty—stepped in front of her, blocking her view of Zane.

"Yes, but first—my mom and Dylan," she said forcefully, finally loosening her jaw enough to speak clearly. She was still shivering, but not as violently. "You need to make sure my mom and nephew are safe."

"I thought of them the second I recognized you out there in the lake. There's an officer on the phone with your mom right now. She's going to keep talking to her until she gets to the house and sees for herself that your mom and nephew are okay."

Caroline released a deep sigh and finally allowed herself to feel a hint of relief.

Matt grabbed an office chair, rolled it close to her and then sat down on it. Now she could see Zane again. He was keeping an eye on her while the EMT took his vitals. Zane raised his eyebrows slightly, his expression matching her own curiosity. Why was he here? How long had he been back in town? He must have the same questions about her.

"Tell me everything that happened," Matt said.

Caroline turned her attention back to him and she described everything she could recall about the attack. "Did you catch either of them?" she asked when she was finished.

He rubbed his hand over his bristly black hair. "Not yet."

"What's this?" the paramedic asked. Now that he'd gotten her warmed up and determined her vital signs were okay, he'd started to check for injuries. He'd pulled back the blanket from the area around her shoulder and seen the rip in her jacket and blouse and the surrounding patch of blood on the fabric.

"I think I got nicked by a bullet."

The paramedic reached into his supply bag for scissors, cut the clothes around her shoulder and got busy cleaning the wound. She could feel him working, but lingering numbness from the cold water blunted the pain.

"Did either of the men say anything that would tell you the motive for the attack?" Matt asked.

She shook her head.

"Well, it didn't involve robbery. We found your purse by the bench where you sat on the upper level. Your wallet and phone were still in it."

"The attack might be connected to the murder of her brother," Zane said.

Matt glanced at Zane, then turned back to Caroline.

"I realize that's the obvious assumption," Caroline said quietly. "But I don't know for sure." Although her brother had been murdered in Seattle, the Cobalt PD had taken an active interest in the case, partly because Owen was a Cobalt resident. But also many of the officers on the force still remembered his father, Sergeant Henry Marsh. They still treated Caroline like family down at the police department even though her father had been killed seven years ago. And they were anxious to do everything they could to help find Owen's killer.

"I'm so sorry about Owen," Zane said, his voice low and husky with emotion.

Caroline didn't respond. She couldn't. Not right now. She'd had enough emotional meltdowns for the time being.

Matt glanced at Zane again and then turned back to her with one eyebrow raised and his lips pursed together. "You two know each other?"

"We used to," Caroline answered, her voice as clipped as she could make it, hoping that Matt would drop this line of questioning.

"Huh." He nodded slightly, seeming to get the hint. "Can you think of anybody else who would want to come after you for any reason?" Matt asked. "You have any kind of feud going on? Do you owe anybody money? Anything like that?"

"No."

The paramedic told her the bullet had torn off a layer of skin and underlying tissue, but that the bone beneath it seemed sound. He wanted her to go to the hospital to get X-rays just to be sure. When she told him she'd knocked her head against the boardwalk and felt strangely sleepy for a minute or two, he definitely wanted her to go and get a thorough check.

Zane stood. "I'll make the trip to the hospital with you. If the ER doctor releases you, I'll see you home."

Oh no, he would not.

"Can you walk okay?" Matt asked. "If you feel up to it, I'd like to get you in a patrol car and away from here as soon as possible. Those men who tried to kill you could be long gone. But they could also be repositioning themselves nearby to take another shot as soon as they can. From what you've described, they sound like hired professionals. If they don't kill you they don't get paid. They're not going to give up easily."

While Matt was talking to Caroline, another uniformed officer walked in carrying a couple of blue nylon gym bags. He tossed one of the bags to Zane. "Temperature's dropping fast. You shouldn't be out walking around in wet clothes. I brought you a pair of jeans and a shirt from your locker at the station." Then the officer walked over to Caroline and handed her the second bag. "Some of the women at the station donated clothes for you, too."

What was going on here?

"Wait a minute," Caroline said as Zane zipped open the bag and started pulling out clothes. "You have a locker at the *police* station?"

He nodded. "I do."

"You can't be a cop," she said, confused.

"It's not my full-time job. I've got other

commitments. But I am a reserve officer. Mostly called out for search and rescue."

Caroline held up her hand for him to stop talking. The conversation was moving way too fast and there were too many gaps in the information she was getting. She needed a second to make sense of it all. "Are you saying you've been back in town for a while?"

"About a year."

"A *year*?" Caroline and her mom had moved back to town a month ago. And nobody had thought to mention that Zane Coleman was back in Cobalt?

Matt caught her attention and gestured at her to hurry up and open the gym bag.

Trying to collect her thoughts, she slowly pulled out a gray sweatshirt and gray sweatpants. Then she looked back at Zane. "Where have you been all these years?"

He drew in a breath and blew it out. "That's a long story."

"We don't have time to listen to it right now," Matt interjected. "Come on. You two need to hurry up and get dressed so we can get Caroline out of here."

The most important thing at the moment was getting Caroline safely out of the office complex and to the hospital.

Zane kept his thoughts focused on that point as he finished changing into dry clothes in one of the insurance broker's inner offices.

But concentrating was a challenge when his mind kept tripping over the fact that Caroline had moved back to town. He'd had no idea.

Six weeks ago he'd seen her sitting in a pew at Owen's funeral while he had stood in the back of the church. His tears had flowed freely at the memory of the flannel-wearing, granola-chomping, nature-loving kid who had followed him around like he was an honorary big brother back when Zane and Caroline started dating.

Zane had wanted to offer his condolences like the other mourners after the graveside service, but showing up unexpectedly at that time and place felt wrong. He couldn't have done that to Caroline and her mom. Mrs. Marsh, once an energetic and outdoorsy woman, had looked shockingly thin and frail. The amount of time from Owen's murder to the funeral hadn't been enough for her to lose that much weight. Something else had to have been going on.

He didn't spend much time in the actual town of Cobalt these days. Instead he spent the majority of his time helping to rebuild the old horse ranch owned by his aunt and uncle.

He probably wouldn't have heard about her return to Cobalt even if he came to town more often. Zane made it a habit to politely walk away from gossip. He had spent too much time on the receiving end of thoughtless comments as a kid, hearing the biting remarks of adults who didn't bother to lower their voice. He had no desire to do that to anybody else.

When he was a kid, his dad worked horses by day and he was good at it. But he was angry at the world after the death of Zane's mother and when he came home at night, he used drugs to feel better. Then he began to sell them. After that, it was a short step to dabbling in other criminal enterprises. Everybody had an opinion about Lee Coleman, and as a kid, Zane got tired of hearing about it. Everyone automatically assumed the worst of him—and for a while he'd been bitter and angry enough to live down to their expectations.

God had clearly been looking out for Zane the day Sergeant Henry Marsh found him selling cans of beer to fellow high school kids at three times their original cost. Zane also happened to have a little bit of weed he'd stolen from his dad stuffed into his shirt pocket. Sergeant Henry had cuffed him and tossed him in the back of his patrol car, and Zane had immediately turned on the charm. He'd learned to flip it on like a light switch as a survival mechanism to get his unstable dad to calm down. It was a useful talent and nearly every adult fell for it. Sergeant Marsh never did.

Neither did his daughter.

Zane stepped back into the office lobby. Caroline had already changed clothes and she had her phone up to her ear. It sounded like she was talking to her mom. Lauren Marsh had always been friendly and kind to Zane. Had even baked a cake and made a big deal about his birthdays.

But that feeling of him being part of their family belonged to the past. And Zane had made himself a promise he would only live life moving forward. Indulging in regret or trying to figure out a way to change things that could never be changed was a waste of time. It didn't help him or anyone else.

He would do everything he could to keep Caroline safe because he owed it to her. And it was something he could do to honor the memories of Sergeant Henry and Owen. But that was it. There was no going back and undoing the mistakes he'd made.

"Who knew you were coming out to your lawyer's office today?" Matt asked Caroline as soon as she disconnected her call.

She thought for a moment. "I couldn't tell you exactly. Probably a lot of people. It wasn't a secret. I've been over here fairly often since…since Owen died."

"Settling your brother's estate?"

She nodded. "And getting everything set up for guardianship of my nephew."

"Any fight over inheritance? Bad feelings? Anything like that?"

Caroline sighed. "Owen's ex-wife, Michelle, is disappointed that she didn't get anything from Owen's estate. I've only talked to her twice, but she's got the impression Owen's business, Wilderness Photo Adventures, is raking in a lot of cash. I told her she's mistaken. There really hasn't been any money flowing in yet. Owen was just getting his company started." Her chin began to tremble and she hurriedly wiped away the tears glistening at the corners of her eyes.

Zane felt his guts twist at the sight of her in so much pain and he took a steadying breath. He wanted to put an arm around her and comfort her, but that was not his place. It hadn't been for a long time.

"I'm sorry, it's kind of hard to think right now." She exhaled a ragged sigh. "Maybe there's something I should have noticed, but didn't."

Matt's phone rang, and he answered it, turning aside.

Caroline faced Zane. "Thank you for helping me. I mean that sincerely. But I don't want you going with me to the hospital. And I don't want to talk to you anywhere else. I have enough drama going on in my life right now."

She had every right to dismiss him. But she also needed to be protected. "I'd like to do what I can to help keep you and your family safe."

She sighed and got her quivering chin under control. "You said you do search and rescue work. Go search for those men who tried to kill us."

As soon as he got the call, he'd be on it. But there was no way he was going to rush in on his own and risk messing up an investigation. "When the police department needs me, they'll call. And I'll do everything I can to help. Right now I'm more concerned with looking out for you."

"No, thank you."

"We found that white van you mentioned," said Matt, disconnecting his phone and turning to them. "Abandoned. It was reported stolen earlier this afternoon." He turned to Zane. "Let's get rolling. I'll finish taking your statement while we're at the hospital."

Caroline cut Zane a sideways glance. She might not want him to come along, but the cop in charge did. And that was good enough for him.

They stepped up to the door and Matt's phone chimed. He opened up a text, hesitated and then held out the phone so Caroline and Zane could see a picture. "They found this in the van." It was a crumpled computer-printed photo of Caroline. "That tells me these guys didn't know you personally. And they didn't act on some bizarre random impulse. This was a contract hit."

Which meant Matt's earlier cautious assumption was right. The gunmen were professionals who had been hired to kill Caroline. They would try again.

THREE

It was well past dark when Caroline stepped out of Cobalt Community Hospital into the crisp, cool air.

The top of her left arm and shoulder were numb thanks to the injection a nurse had given her prior to receiving a half dozen stitches. The doctor confirmed no bones were broken and that, in spite of knocking her head on the boardwalk, her skull and everything inside of it checked out okay.

She could have been admitted overnight for observation, but she didn't want to stay any longer than she had to. She was anxious to get back to the house. Even though she'd spoken to both her mom and Dylan on the phone, she still wanted to see for herself that they were okay.

Zane walked beside her, constantly sweeping his gaze across their surroundings. Matt walked ahead, his holster unbuckled and his hand resting on his service revolver.

"Any updates on the search for those creeps who tried to kill us?" She directed her question to Matt. It had been a couple of hours since she last talked to him or to Zane. She had given her statement to a detective, and a female officer she'd never met before had guarded the examining room while she was getting checked out by the doctor.

"Forensics is still going over the van," Matt answered without turning around. "We've got officers canvassing the neighborhood where it was originally stolen as well as the area where it was ditched. And we're interviewing witnesses, taking descriptions and having people look at mug shots. We'll have you take a look at them after you've gotten some rest."

Matt's patrol car was at the end of a short walkway outside a secondary entrance at the back of the hospital. The plan was to keep her departure as low-key as possible. A second patrol car idled behind Matt's, with two officers standing outside the vehicles, keeping an eye on the few cars driving by on the narrow street.

Cobalt was a small mountain town that had experienced a population explosion after being featured in several outdoor living online magazines and television shows over the last few years. The high-end Cobalt Resort had gone up on the edge of the lake, its owners hoping to capitalize on people's love of pristine nature combined with luxury accommodations.

Staffing the resort had significantly added to the town's population above and beyond the tourists, which led to far too many people for the authorities to keep in check. City services were struggling to keep up and the police department was stretched thin. They had enough problems on their hands without giving Caroline a personal escort and the assurance of round-the-clock armed babysitters for at least the next twenty-four hours.

"I think Matt can probably get me home safely," Caroline said to Zane as they reached the end of the walkway. "You might as well head on home. And thank you, again."

He looked down at the hand she'd extended to him and then up into her eyes. He lifted an eyebrow. "You want to shake hands and say good-bye?"

"You saved my life today." Her voice wavered a little and she cleared her throat. "You don't need to do anything else."

On the ride from the office complex to the hospital she'd formed a long mental list of questions for him. But she'd held back on asking any of them. It didn't seem like the right time or place. Then, while she was in the hospital's treatment room, she'd thought about how much she truly deserved answers. And apologies. It was just a step beyond that to deciding that no apology would ever be sufficient; no explanation would make up for the pain he had caused her. She'd focused her energy on building up her anger for Zane because that was more tolerable than facing the dark, twisting fear for herself and her family that threatened to overwhelm her.

Anger felt less threatening right now. And she had a right to be angry. Her entire family had welcomed him into the fold. They all had loved him. Or thought they did. Obviously he hadn't been the person they had believed he was. After all, he had decided to leave town rather than stay and face his criminal father. He could have assisted the Cobalt police department, but he had chosen not to. Which made it especially strange that he was employed by them as a reserve officer now.

She'd worked herself into a pretty good snit while getting her shoulder patched up, telling herself that he probably wouldn't even be there in the waiting room when the doctor was finished. That he would have abandoned her again. But there he was. And at the sight of him she felt something like an arrow pierce her being.

She wasn't happy to see him. She couldn't be. She decided she was annoyed that he hadn't left her side like she'd asked when they'd departed the office complex. Yes, he saved her life and she was truly grateful. But his staying around made everything more miserable and complicated. It stirred up memories and feelings she wanted to keep neatly tucked away. She didn't want to yell at him or argue with him. She just wanted to be done with him—the way she thought she had been for all those years.

It was on the tip of her tongue to confirm that she really did want him to go away as they stood at the end of the walkway. But then she thought of something she'd always heard but truly learned only after her father's death. She'd been reminded of the same lesson again after Owen's passing—life is short. And fragile. We can't afford to hold on to our grudges as long as we'd like to. The time to forgive is now.

She took a deep breath, blew it out and felt her body relax just a little. Sure, she may not be ready to forgive quite yet, but she could at least be polite and give him an explanation.

"Look, my mom's already upset," she said in a calmer tone. "She doesn't need the shock of seeing you right now after all these years. It'll just make things worse."

"What happened with your mom?" Zane asked gently. "Has she been ill?"

Caroline hesitated. It wasn't something she wanted to talk about right now.

"I'll stay outside of the house," he quickly added. "I'll make sure your mom doesn't see me." He cleared his throat. "Please let me help you. It's something I can do for Owen."

She felt a pang in her heart. "He loved you like a brother."

"I felt the same way." Zane rubbed his chin. "We crossed paths and I spoke to him a couple of times after I came back to Cobalt."

Caroline felt her jaw slacken and for a few seconds she was speechless. "I can't believe he didn't tell me." She shook her head. Why would Owen keep that from her?

"It was only twice. And the first conversation went pretty rough." A half smile flashed across his face. "Owen wasn't a kid anymore. And he was very protective of you. Didn't want to tell me where you were. Told me he would let you know he saw me and find out if you wanted to talk to me before he'd share a word about you. But I think he wanted to get a handle on me first before letting you know."

Her little brother had thought he needed to take care of her? Ridiculous.

And touching. Owen had been carrying more of a burden on his shoulders than she'd realized. Weathering a painful divorce after being abandoned by his wife. Summoning all the emotion and patience and energy it took to raise a small boy while starting his own business. And maybe getting dragged into something else that had gotten him killed.

Zane was watching her intently, waiting for her response.

"I guess it would be all right if you came along on this one ride out to the house," she said. "Just stay out of view of my mom and my nephew. And afterward you stay away from all of us."

"If that's what you want."

They reached Matt's patrol car. He had Caroline sit in the back seat with Zane beside her. One of the officers that had been watching the street slipped into the front passenger seat. He introduced himself as Shane, but didn't say anything more.

A shiver passed through Caroline as they pulled away from the hospital. The life she'd carefully built in California had started unraveling the moment she'd heard Owen was murdered. Now someone was trying to kill *her*. She also had her mom and nephew relying on her and no idea what to do next.

She glanced out the window at the disappearing lights of town as they followed the curving road along the lake. The Cobalt Resort shone like a golden beacon and reflected on the rippling surface of the dark water. After a couple of miles the road became a highway and turned away into the forest. Caroline blew out a breath. *Please, Lord, keep Dylan and Mom safe. And help me know what to do.*

Zane had had plenty of experience with night patrols in enemy territory. At least this transport of Caroline along an Idaho highway wasn't being conducted on foot. And the chances of coming across an improvised explosive device were pretty slim.

On the other hand, they had little protection. No helmets. No body armor. No air support to fall back on.

Yeah, he was overthinking things. He knew it. It was a post-combat survival instinct that would likely never go away. That's what the therapist told him when he'd sought help six months after returning from his second tour in Afghanistan, after he'd found himself unable to drive past a broken-down car by the side of the road or anything else that looked like a potential trap. Anything and everything out of the ordinary made him wary.

He'd had a lot to talk about that first year after he'd returned to civilian life, staying with friends near the base where he'd been stationed in North Carolina. Most of it was related to combat, but some of it went back to things that had happened before he'd even enlisted.

The headlights of their patrol car cut through the darkness and shone on the curving road ahead. Cobalt was in mountain country, barely seventy miles south of the Canadian border. The deep mountain lake, for which the town was named, was surrounded by heavily forested jagged mountain peaks.

Owen's house was located in a small community south of the lake. They were modest homes, mostly occupied by people who worked in the Cobalt Resort, downtown restaurants or the local ski resort.

Zane kept his gaze sweeping across the surrounding terrain as he'd been trained. Not that he could see much looking out into the darkness. The police radio crackled with regular transmissions. Routine stuff, mostly about traffic stops. So far he'd heard little related to the search for the men who'd attacked him and Caroline. But he also knew any substantial information would likely be transmitted by cell phone so anyone with a scanner couldn't listen in.

Matt asked Shane a question and they started talking.

"So, where have you been all this time?" Caroline asked quietly from beside him.

Zane wasn't looking to keep secrets. Not anymore. And Caroline deserved answers.

"I was in Texas for a little while. A couple of other places, and then Afghanistan."

"So were you in military? A private contractor?"

"Army."

"It makes sense now," she said thoughtfully. "That explains how you got the skills to help in the police reserves." She was studying his face. He could see her in the light from the instrument panel in the front seat and, for a couple of seconds, from the bright beams of a passing car. "It explains why you look so different, too," she added.

"The passage of time will do that." He felt self-conscious, wondering exactly what kind of changes she saw.

"That isn't the only thing that changes a person."

She was right.

"When you said we needed time apart, that you were going to leave town for a while, everybody thought you'd just be gone for a few weeks. Maybe a couple of months. Why didn't you tell us that you were leaving to join the military? That you were going to be gone a long time?" She glanced at the two officers up front who were still carrying on their conversation. "Why didn't you tell *me*?"

The catch in her voice made the center of his chest ache. At the time he'd had no doubt she'd get over him after he left. That he wasn't anybody special. But he'd also known she had a kind heart and might worry about him for a little while. If he'd told her what he was planning at the time, she might have tried to convince him not to go. And he would have been very tempted to listen to her.

Sitting in a patrol car with a couple of cops wasn't exactly the place where he wanted to talk to her about the past, but what choice did he have? She'd said this ride to the house was the only time he'd have with her. If he was going to wrap up any unanswered questions for her, he had to do it now. And at least for the moment, Matt and Shane were focused on their own conversation.

"I'm sure you remember the increase in

drug crime about the time I left," he said. "Suppliers fighting over territory."

"Remember it?" She made a scoffing sound. "My dad got killed in the middle of it."

Zane didn't say anything for a few seconds. Didn't trust himself to talk about the man who'd been like a real father to him without breaking down. Caroline didn't need that right now. She needed someone strong she could lean on.

"Did you know he'd been shot?" Caroline asked.

"Yes." Zane had been through basic training and shipped overseas by the time he'd heard— word had taken a while to reach him. And he hadn't known how to react once he'd heard. There was a lot going on in his life at the time. The death of Sergeant Henry Marsh had been one very significant addition to a long list of emotional events he couldn't deal with just then. He'd unpacked the pain of that loss a few years later, when his life had threatened to get out of control and he'd needed to face everything he'd been avoiding for so long. That was when he'd finally seen a therapist.

"Why didn't you call us?" she asked. Her voice was cold and hard. "Send a card? *Something?* Did you know my mom had a heart attack shortly after it happened, leaving serious damage? That's why Owen set up his estate with a request that I take care of Dylan instead of Mom." Caroline shook her head. "She would have been the logical choice. She knows what she's doing. But she doesn't have the strength to take care of him full time until he's an adult."

So that was why Mrs. Marsh had looked so frail at Owen's funeral.

"I'm sorry about your mom. And I'm sorry I didn't call after your dad… I guess I just thought calling after leaving the way I did would make things about me at a time when they needed to be about your family." One more thing he hadn't handled well. But not because he hadn't cared. Quite the opposite.

"A few days before I left, my dad showed up at my apartment in the middle of the night," Zane said. "He told me things were changing around Cobalt and that some new business associates were going to make him rich. But they weren't interested in working with a guy whose son was involved with a cop's family. Told me it would be best for everyone if I left town."

The conversation had gotten loud and ugly. Lee Coleman had been using too much of the stuff he was selling, and as a result he'd lost his job at the horse ranch where he'd worked and lived for years. The drugs made him paranoid and it had been clear he was afraid Zane would sell him out to the police.

"When he told me bad things would happen to you, your family, anyone I cared about if I didn't get out of town, I knew I had to go. I didn't start thinking about the military until a couple of weeks after I left. I was afraid if I called to tell you, once I heard your voice I'd change my mind and come back. And that would put you right back into danger again."

He rubbed his hand over his face. This was old history. And it would be good to get it wrapped up so he could move on. Returning to Cobalt wasn't about trying to relive the past. It was about pursuing his dream of working with horses. He had the opportunity to do that here. Forget trying to recapture things that he'd lost or ruined. Indulging in wishful thinking like that had made his life miserable for far too long.

"So you left when you could have stayed and helped send your dad to prison?" Caroline prompted. The anger was gone from her tone. Now she sounded aloof. Like she really didn't want anything else to do with him.

"The local cops had started forming a task force with state and federal agencies around the time I left. I met with a couple of detectives and told them everything I knew. They asked that I not tell anyone about that meeting in order to keep my dad from finding out and retaliating."

His dad hadn't been involved in the Marsh shooting. But he did get busted for selling drugs and served five years in prison down in Boise. While Zane hadn't been able to protect Sergeant Henry, at least leaving town had kept Caroline and the rest of the family safe.

A disquieting thought flickered in Zane's mind. Could his father have had something to do with today's attack? Zane hadn't heard from him in years. The odds were good that he was back in Cobalt. Other than the time spent in prison, he'd never lived anywhere else.

Caroline was quiet for a moment. "Why didn't you tell *my* dad what was happening? Why didn't you stay here and let us stand by you?"

Why? Because his own dad had warned him against doing just that and had told him the same thing he always did. That Zane was his son and just like him. That the Marsh family were a completely different kind of people. Nice. Law-abiding. Churchgoing. That Zane might be able to fool them into accepting him in the short term, but in the long run they'd see what he really was. That he wasn't worth the trouble. It was Zane's deepest fear: he was unworthy of love. And his drug-addled dad spoke right to it.

It had taken several more years in his faith walk for Zane to be able to believe he had value simply as a child of God. Though he still had moments—sometimes whole days— when he struggled to believe that.

Caroline watched him closely, still waiting for a response.

He had been twenty years old when he'd left town, desperate to protect the young woman he loved. Of course if the same thing happened now, he would make very different decisions. Zane drew in a deep breath and blew it out. "I guess I just figured you and your family didn't need the headache."

Caroline stared at him for what felt like a very long time and then slowly shook her head. An expression of pained disappointment seemed to darken her eyes. "After everything my parents did for you? After everything you and I talked about and the life we planned together? I can't believe that."

There was nothing more for Zane to say.

Her response was a good reminder of why things would never have worked out between the two of them. Even when she tried, she couldn't understand him. They'd had such different starts in life. Been brought up so differently. And there was no overcoming that.

FOUR

"Remember—you agreed to stay out of sight when we got here." Caroline glanced at Zane and then back at her brother's house as Matt pulled his patrol car to the curb. He parked behind the police cruiser that had already been dispatched to the house to protect Dylan and Caroline's mom, Lauren, right after the attack on Caroline. Shane got out and walked over to talk to the officer already on the scene. Matt got on the radio to let dispatch know they'd arrived.

"So, you didn't mention me at all to your mom when you talked to her on the phone while we were at the hospital?" Zane asked quietly.

Despite everything, Caroline felt the tug of a slight emotional connection to him. There would be a lot to sort through when her thoughts settled down. But she was determined to keep her feelings toward Zane buried. Right now she had her mom and nephew to take care of and keep safe. And a business to run. And she needed to stay alive. Those were her priorities.

"Telling her I almost got killed was enough stress for her to handle for one day. I didn't think we needed to drudge up sad old memories of you vanishing without a trace on top of that."

"Understood."

He sounded matter-of-fact. But even after all these years apart, she knew him well enough to hear the disappointment he was trying to hide.

"When the time is right I'll tell her about what you did for me and that you're back in Cobalt. Hopefully, that will happen before she bumps into you at a store or something."

Matt finished his radio call, tapped something into his computer and then twisted around to glance at the back seat. "You two sit tight. I want to take a quick look around the exterior of the house and then I'll walk Caroline up to the door. I'll call your mom and tell her it's me so I don't scare her."

"Okay. Thank you."

He grabbed a flashlight and got out of the car. In the glow from the headlights she could see him make a quick phone call. After he pocketed his phone, he flicked on the flashlight and started around a corner of the house.

Caroline took a moment to tuck her hair behind her ears and straighten her shirt. It was important to give her mom and Dylan the impression that she was fine and everything was under control. She glanced at the house, feeling a little queasy at the thought she very easily might not have lived to see the end of this day. *Thank You, Lord.*

"Do you live nearby?" she asked Zane. What she really wanted to ask him was how likely it would be that they'd run into each other.

"I live on a horse ranch about twelve miles northwest of town." The seat made a slight squeaking sound as he turned toward her. "Do you remember me ever mentioning my mom's brother, Jack?"

"I don't remember the name." Her voice shook and her hands started to tremble for no apparent reason. She tucked them under her thighs so she could keep them still. It was probably just nerves over what had happened to her today. Maybe the shock of the whole experience was wearing off. She'd thought it already had. But maybe the emotional impact of something like that wasn't so simple. Somebody had tried to *kill* her.

Her stomach began to feel like it was tying itself into a knot. Talking to Zane on the ride over must have distracted and calmed her more than she'd realized. But now that she was home and things were quieting down, the reality of today's horrifying experience was catching up with her.

"Uncle Jack and his wife, Rose, bought the ranch property years ago," Zane continued, not giving any indication if he'd noticed that Caroline was on the verge of some kind of meltdown. "They lived in Denver when I was growing up. They'd planned to move back here for years, but being able to do it took longer than they had expected.

"I got an email from Aunt Rose while I was over in Afghanistan. The USO helped her find me. I hadn't heard from her or my uncle in years. We got reacquainted and when I returned to civilian life they offered me the chance to buy into the horse ranch. Getting everything up and going on their own was too much for them."

It helped that Zane continued to talk about something so normal in such a soothing tone. It made her feel calmer. Maybe that was his intention.

Though they weren't touching, his strong physical presence felt comforting so close to her. She reminded herself they were basically strangers to each other now. And it would be best if they kept it that way.

"Well, it sounds like you live far enough away that Mom probably won't bump into you." Caroline's voice was back to normal. That trembling attack, whatever it was, seemed to be over. For now.

"And I'll make sure I stay out of view while I'm here tonight."

She gave him a sideways glance. "What are you talking about?"

"I'm going to stay here and help Matt keep an eye on things."

She nodded her head toward the patrol car parked in front of them. "I thought that officer was going to take you back to town after I got home safely."

He lifted a shoulder in a slight shrug. "He's going to take Shane back so he can return to patrol and help look for the bad guys. Matt and I will stay here."

She didn't want to think about how vulnerable she and Mom and Dylan were out here in this little house. She wanted to believe the men who tried to kill her were long gone—but that would be naïve. These were hired killers. They wouldn't give up that easily. Still…

"Do you really think there needs to be two of you here?"

"What happened today was a pretty brazen attack. The chief of police thinks we're better off being especially cautious."

Caroline nodded. She was exhausted. But at the same time she couldn't imagine getting a wink of sleep tonight.

"Is that your mom's car?" Zane gestured at a sedan parked in the driveway. "I know you left Owen's SUV at the office complex, by the way. I'll make sure it gets back to you tomorrow."

"That car belongs to an old friend of my mom's. Her name's Rennie."

Caroline heard Owen's dog barking in the house. Matt reappeared around the corner of the garage and walked over to the patrol car. "All right, everything looks good. Nobody lurking in the bushes. Let's get you into the house."

Before they went their separate ways Caroline glanced at Zane, feeling like she wanted to say something but having no idea what it should be.

He gave her a slight nod, like he understood. Then she got out of the car.

Matt walked beside her to the front door. The fear that Zane had helped her keep under control was fighting its way to the surface again and her knees started to shake. But, conscious of how she wanted to appear to Dylan, she took a deep breath and forced herself to hold it together for just a little longer.

The front door opened before she even reached the steps. Her gaze immediately fell on a little boy with dark blond hair falling into his eyes. He held a battered plush tiger in his hands, twisting it slightly as if he were anxious. The poor kid often looked anxious these days.

Then Caroline saw her mom. Her hair was the same color as Dylan's, but shorter and neater. Lauren Marsh wasn't a tall woman. She used to be nearly as round as the chocolate truffles she liked to make at Christmas, but she'd rapidly lost weight after Caroline's father was killed and she'd been slender ever since.

Millie, Owen's Australian shepherd and mystery dog mix, wriggled between Mom and Dylan. Caroline stepped over the threshold and in an instant she was enveloped in hugs and getting her shin licked by the dog.

Matt stayed outside and closed the door.

Her mom held on to her for a long time. When she finally let go and wiped the tears from her eyes, Lauren's friend, Rennie, stepped forward to give Caroline a quick hug and said, "We've been praying for you."

Dylan, who hadn't been told what had happened but who must have picked up on the tension from the grown-ups, gave her a welcoming smile. She dropped down to her knees and hugged him, holding him a little longer than usual. Then she got back to her feet, relieved to see that her family was okay.

Her mom stepped forward to brush the hair from Caroline's face and tuck it behind her ear. "We can talk a little later if you need to." She glanced at Dylan, then went back to fussing with Caroline's hair. "You must be tired."

"I am."

"Good thing Zane was there to help you."

"Huh?" Caroline's jaw dropped. At the end of a day when she thought she couldn't possibly be shocked any further, she raised her eyebrows and stared at her mom, unable to speak.

The hint of an impish smile lifted one corner of Lauren's mouth and brought a little bit of humor to her eyes despite the somber situation. "Being Sergeant Marsh's widow still has some influence in Cobalt. I've been getting calls throughout the day." She gestured toward the house phone on the countertop. "The last person who called said it looked like

Zane was going to stay by your side until you got home. Is he in one of the cars out there?"

"Yes."

Her mom walked to the door and opened it. "Be right back." She stepped outside and closed the door behind her.

Caroline started to follow her, and Rennie put a hand on her shoulder. "You should probably stay inside."

Caroline turned to Dylan. He was rubbing his eyes. She gave him the biggest smile she could muster and picked him up, trying not to use the shoulder that had been injured. He rested his head against her neck. It was past his normal bedtime. "I missed you while I was gone, buddy."

"I missed you, too," he said sleepily.

Caroline walked over to a window, moved the curtain slightly to one side and watched as Lauren walked up to Matt's patrol car and stood outside the passenger door. Zane opened the door and got out. He stood with his arms held stiffly at his sides, like he was ready for a dressing-down. Her mom waited for just a second before she stepped forward and wrapped her arms around his broad chest for a hug. He was tall and she was fairly short so that was about as far as she could reasonably reach.

Zane hesitated, then turned his head slightly

and leaned down so his ear rested on the top of her head. Caroline felt a lump form in her throat. They had all been so close once. And so much had happened since the last time they'd been together.

Her mom released her hold on him, turned, appeared to say something Caroline couldn't hear and then headed up the driveway. Zane followed. When they opened the front door Caroline realized she was holding her breath and blew it out. Zane locked gazes with her, then looked at Dylan. She was pretty certain the boy was asleep in her arms. Millie didn't wag her tail, but she didn't growl, either. Zane held out his hand and the dog took a sniff and let him scratch her head.

After introductions between Rennie and Zane, Rennie said it was time for her to head home. She grabbed her purse from the kitchen counter and left.

"Don't worry, honey," Lauren said to Zane as soon as the door closed behind Rennie. "I'm not going to ask you about your personal business. I just wanted to get a good look at you in the light. And I wanted to thank you for what you did today."

Zane glanced at Caroline. He looked tired, with dark circles forming under his eyes. It struck her that she'd nearly forgotten he'd almost been killed, too.

He cleared his throat. "I'm just grateful I was there."

"The Lord has His plans."

"Yes, ma'am. I count on that."

"Have you had time to eat today?" she continued. "I remember Matt from when he first joined the department. He can come in or I can fix something for the two of you to eat out in the car."

Caroline bit her lower lip to keep from snapping at her mom. She understood that her mom was nervous and anxious and relieved, all at the same time. But she was also acting like the past had never taken place—as if they were going to renew their relationship with Zane, which was not going to happen. He'd moved on. Everybody had moved on. Mom had to accept that.

"Thank you, but I ate while we were at the hospital," Zane said to Caroline's relief. "And I'm sure you could all use some rest."

"Yes," Caroline said, hoping to get him out the door before her mom could drag this out further. Her injured shoulder was starting to ache. The numbing medication must be wearing off, and exhaustion was settling in throughout her whole body. She should probably hand Dylan over to her mom, but she didn't want to. "Thank you again, for everything."

Zane moved to the door and turned toward Caroline just before he opened it. "Lock the door behind me. Make sure all the doors and windows are locked."

"I will."

He stepped out and closed the door behind him, waiting on the step until he heard Caroline slide the deadbolt into place. Then he walked away.

She hugged Dylan a little bit tighter. The world had become a frightening place. She wondered if she'd ever feel safe again.

Zane watched a pair of headlights snake around a corner and head down the road toward him as he sat in the patrol car. He looked at the screen on his phone. Just after 2:00 a.m. Closing time at the bars. Maybe it was somebody headed home after having a couple of drinks. Or somebody getting off work after serving them.

He glanced over at Owen's house. Light glowed from a couple of windows and he wondered if Caroline had left them on. If she was still awake.

Or maybe she'd left them on for reassurance

so she could sleep. He'd done that. More than once, he'd found himself trying to get some rest at the end of a day when some thought or memory would trigger a dream and he'd be back in Afghanistan again. He'd awaken terrified, sweating, trying to make his way through those awful disorienting few seconds when he couldn't remember the date or where he was—couldn't recall which of his buddies had made it back home and which had departed from this life for good. Afterward, he'd left the lights on. It'd helped a little.

The headlights crept closer. The person driving the vehicle could be heading for any of the six houses in Zane's line of sight. There was no reason to believe the driver was coming to *this* house.

But given what had happened today, he listened to the unease that gnawed at him.

He nudged Matt in the seat beside him. The cop's eyes were open and he was sitting up in an instant. "What have we got?" Matt asked.

"Might not be anything."

Matt had likely never fallen asleep, but Zane had encouraged him to get some rest while Zane kept watch. The sergeant had already worked a regular shift, plus he had young kids at home who would need his energy later on. No doubt they'd be awake and bouncing off the walls when the sun came up and their dad was trying to catch up on some sleep before going back to work again.

Matt turned on the car's engine and called dispatch to report the situation.

Zane could see now that it was a pickup truck heading toward them. Big, new, with flashy accessories.

"That rig looks familiar." Matt started to tap the plate numbers into his computer as the truck came to a stop in the middle of the road a few feet ahead of them. They could hear yelling from inside the cab despite the deep rumbling of the engine, but they couldn't get a clear view inside.

The passenger door flew open and a woman scrambled out. Skinny, in a short black sparkly dress and spike heels. Aiming a rude gesture toward the driver of the truck, she marched across the street and continued across the lawn and up toward the front door of Owen's house.

"I got her." Zane was already halfway out of the car.

Matt nodded. "I'll watch the truck."

Zane jogged up behind the woman. The scents of stale beer and cigarette smoke trailed after her.

"Ma'am," Zane called out, coming up alongside her. "Hold up a minute. Can I talk to you?"

"Don't think you cops are going to keep me from my baby," she snarled without slowing down.

So this was Michelle, Owen's former wife? Dylan's mom?

"Dylan is fine," Zane said, trying to quiet her down before she woke up everybody in the house.

He couldn't tell if she was drunk or high or if she was just plain selfish and obnoxious. It was hard to imagine a decent, smart guy like Owen had ever been married to a woman like this. But then Zane had his own life scars to prove he didn't always make the best decisions, either. He stepped in front of her as she raised her fist to pound on the front door.

Blowing out a huff of annoyance, she jammed her fist into her hip. She held a phone with the other. "My baby could have gotten killed today and I need to see him!"

"I'm sure he's asleep," Zane said. Dylan had looked to be already asleep before, though maybe not anymore with all the racket on the front porch.

"Well, somebody can wake him up. He can sleep later. That's all he does, anyway." She tapped the screen on her phone a couple of times, lifted it to her ear, paused, then said, "Yeah, I'm here and I want to see my boy. *Now.*"

A few seconds later Caroline peered through the glass panel beside the door and then opened it. She was dressed in sweatpants and a T-shirt. Her hair was disheveled and she looked exhausted. "You can see Dylan later," she said to Michelle, keeping her voice lowered.

"How do I know he's all right?"

"He's fine. He was home with my mom all day."

"Well, I got here as soon as I heard what happened."

She was likely at a bar when she heard about the shooting, Zane guessed. And she'd waited until after closing time to check on her son.

Michelle leaned over to peer past Caroline's shoulder and look inside the house. "This used to be *my* house, you know. *I* should have gotten it in Owen's will. I should have gotten the business, too. I was there at the very beginning, when it was just a stupid dream of his.

"I know my boy inherited some of this, too," she continued. "*My* boy. Now that his daddy's gone, I should be looking after him and his interests. Not you."

Caroline's face became even paler and her eyes started to look watery.

Cold fury settled in Zane's gut and he took a deep breath. He knew it wasn't his place to interfere, but this was too much. Caroline had already been through more than enough.

"Come back later," he said to Michelle.

She took a step away from him but kept her gaze on Caroline and arched an eyebrow. "I gave Owen custody of my son. Now that his daddy is gone, I could probably get it back. Especially since somebody's trying to kill you. Being around you is putting my son in danger." A slight smile passed over her bright red lips. "Maybe you're not so squeaky clean after all. Tell me, Caroline, what have you been up to that would make somebody come after you like that?"

Caroline hugged herself. "I don't know."

Matt walked up. "This is not the time or place for this conversation."

A tall man in fashionably ripped jeans and a shiny gold shirt had walked up alongside the sergeant. "He's right, baby," the driver of the truck said to Michelle. "Let's get out of here."

Michelle looked at her friend and scowled. Then she glanced at Matt. "All right, I'll go." She turned to Caroline. "But I'll be back to see my boy. And we can talk more about settling accounts."

Zane felt anger burn across the surface of his skin. Her threat was clear. Money. She wanted money or she'd go to court to take Dylan.

"Bill Perry," Matt said as the three of them watched the couple walk back to the truck and then rumble off into the darkness. "I knew I recognized the truck. He's been in and out of jail a few times. Drugs. Possession of stolen goods."

Caroline wore a stoic expression on her face, but tears rolled down her cheeks.

"Is everything all right?" Lauren Marsh called out from inside the house.

Caroline let go of the door to hurriedly wipe at her eyes, and it swung open. Zane could see Mrs. Marsh holding Dylan, his hair sticking out in every direction, shirt riding up to expose a chubby tummy and his thumb stuck in his mouth. The dog, Millie, walked up to the doorway and kept a watchful eye on Zane as she posted herself beside Caroline's feet.

"We need to get Dylan settled down and back to bed," Caroline said wearily. "But thank you, both."

Zane nodded. "Good night."

"Good night," Matt added.

She closed the door. The two men turned and walked down the driveway to the patrol car.

Zane hoped Caroline was as tough as her old man had been. She was going to have to be.

FIVE

Caroline went back to bed after her late-night conversation with her former sister-in-law, but she didn't sleep a wink. She tossed and turned, reliving the terrifying events of the day and thinking about Michelle's promise to settle accounts. Caroline knew exactly what that meant. If she wanted to keep her nephew safely under her roof, she'd have to come up with cash to pay Michelle as quickly as possible.

When the darkness of night started to wear off just before sunrise, she got out of bed and went into the kitchen to make coffee. She had a pounding headache and downed a couple of aspirins. Then she unplugged her charging phone and saw a reminder that she had an appointment she could not cancel. Not if she wanted to pay Michelle and hang on to Dylan.

"Good morning, honey." Caroline's mom trudged into the kitchen, turned on the electric kettle so she could make her instant decaf and then reached down and pulled her waffle iron out of a cabinet. "Why don't you see if Matt and Zane want to come in for some breakfast? I have Matt's number in my phone."

"Sure. I'll send a text." In the text, she asked for Zane to meet her at the picnic table in the backyard. She was pretty sure of what his reaction would be when she told him she needed to go in to the Wilderness Photo Adventures office this morning for a meeting. And she didn't need him to argue with her in front of her mom and get Lauren upset. Or potentially upset Dylan when he woke up.

Right now attending that meeting was a chance she had to take, even if she'd rather stay home and hide under the covers. But she couldn't afford to only think about keeping herself safe. Owen had entrusted her with his son, and Dylan's safety and future were what was most important. That meant she needed to be able to provide for him—and make enough money to keep Dylan's mother away.

"I'm going to take my coffee and go out on the back patio for a few minutes," she said to her mom.

"Okay. I'll let you know when breakfast is ready."

Caroline walked through the swinging door

into the living room and opened the sliding door to step out onto the patio. She stopped beside the picnic table, looking out at the towering tree-covered mountains that surrounded the valley and at the golden morning sunlight that brushed the highest peaks. Life was such a fragile thing. And no one was guaranteed they would see another sunrise. But you had to live your life as if you would. And Caroline *had* to make a success of Owen's business.

She was halfway through her coffee when Zane stepped out onto the patio, sliding the door closed behind him, and walked up beside her. "Good morning. How'd you sleep?"

She shrugged, refusing to complain when he'd spent that same night stuck in a patrol car. For the same reason she really didn't want to start an argument, but she had to get this over with. "I have to go into the office today and I'm going to need someone from the police department to accompany me."

He shook his head. "I checked in with the station before I came up to the house. Neither of the goons who tried to kill you has been arrested, and there are no new leads on them. This is not the time to set up meetings."

"I didn't just set it up. I completely forgot about it until the reminder showed up on my phone this morning." Caroline fought to keep the irritated tone out of her voice. It wasn't his fault her temples were pounding. But she wanted him to know she wasn't being careless or foolhardy. "As you can imagine, I've been distracted by other things," she said into her coffee mug before taking a sip.

"Reschedule."

She looked at him over the rim of her mug. A hint of a beard had appeared on his face. It enhanced his already ruggedly handsome appearance. Just what she needed.

"I've already rescheduled twice over the last couple of weeks. And this morning I saw a text from the man I'm supposed to be meeting. He arrived in town last night."

"If you tell him what happened, I'm sure he'll understand."

"Hey!" Dylan opened the sliding door and ran outside, still in his pajamas and carrying a big plastic ball. Millie trotted by his side and let out a single *woof* to express her own excitement.

Caroline felt some of the tension drain from her shoulders. She'd imagined the little boy spending a night as tormented as she was. But apparently the unexpected appearance of his mom had rolled right off of him. But then he probably had no idea who she was.

Zane asked for Dylan's ball, dropped it to

the grass and then kicked it, starting an impromptu soccer match. Of course he stayed
close to Dylan, making it easy for the boy and
encouraging him when his attempts to kick
the ball didn't quite work out. Millie hovered
nearby, barking her encouragement a couple
of times.

Autumn felt like it had decided to dip back
into summer this morning. Caroline sat at the
picnic table, watching Zane play with Dylan
and knowing her conversation with him
wasn't over. But for now she just enjoyed the
moment. She was determined to do more of
that from now on. At least as much as she
could while someone was trying to kill her.

The match didn't last long. Dylan grabbed
his ball and raced back into the house with
Millie at his heels. Zane walked over to the
picnic table, sat down on the bench beside
Caroline and turned to her.

She lifted a hand to forestall whatever argument he was going to make. "Do you follow winter sports?"

"If something's on TV and it looks interesting I'll watch. Otherwise, not really. I like
to get out and do stuff but I don't follow the
sports celebrities."

"Well, Bobby Boom is a huge name in winter sports in the northwest. Extreme snow-

boarding shows online and specials on cable. Network commentary spots. Big corporate endorsement deals plus his own destination outdoor equipment shops in Seattle, Portland and Vancouver. Can you imagine the business he could bring into Owen's company if we work out some kind of sponsorship deal?"

"That money's not going to do you any good if you're dead."

"Yeah, well, that money might help me keep custody of Dylan if I can pass some of it on to Michelle."

He shook his head. "You're tired and you aren't thinking clearly."

She blew out a puff of air. "You're tired, too. And maybe you don't understand the situation I'm dealing with."

"I'm not that tired," he said mildly. "I got two hours of sleep last night while Matt kept watch. I'm fine. Fresh as a daisy."

Dylan ran back into the yard again. Seeing his wide smile and hearing his squealing laughter as he played with his dog both soothed Caroline's spirits and cut her to the quick at the same time. She loved her nephew more than she could imagine. And she couldn't afford to make a mistake that would hurt him. Having a child depend on her was a relatively new experience, and already she found herself wondering how people dealt with the worry and fear of parenting without having a nervous breakdown.

Caroline's mom came to the back door and called for Dylan to come in and wash up for breakfast. He took off running again.

"Michelle's boyfriend has a criminal record," Zane said once the boy was in the house.

"Owen told me about that."

Zane shook his head. "How did your brother end up married to Michelle? How did they even meet? I'd heard that your family moved away from here."

Caroline crossed her arms. Now that her headache was finally gone, she realized her injured shoulder hurt a little bit. "We moved down to California to be near my mom's family after Dad died. Owen hated to leave and couldn't wait to get back up here. When he was twenty, Mom gave him the portion of Dad's insurance money she'd saved for him. He wanted to start his own business, something to do with the outdoors.

"Somehow he was able to borrow enough money to buy this house. It looked like things were falling into place for him and he got too excited, starting to rush into things—like a relationship with Michelle." She uncrossed her arms and leaned back a little. "They got married three months after they met, apparently before they really knew each other. Sometimes I think meeting her was the biggest mistake of his life. But then I see Dylan and I know that's not true."

"Do you think the attack on you was related to Owen's business?"

Caroline shook her head. "I don't know why it would be. For one thing, it's been shuttered for the last month and earning no money. In that time, most of the buzz and interest Owen was working to generate has died down. We're basically going to have to start Wilderness Photo Adventures all over again. He planned on offering some kayaking and snowshoeing experiences, stuff like that, but mainly it was about getting people out to see the beautiful wilderness around here. Working in some photography help and tips so they'd be happy taking home pictures as mementos and leaving everything else undisturbed.

"He had some sporting equipment, but it's not like he had a ton of valuable inventory. He wasn't making a lot of money. Wilderness Photo Adventures wasn't even completely up and running yet."

"Hey, breakfast is ready," Matt called to them from the back door. He must have stayed inside and talked with Mom while Zane came out to talk to Caroline.

"Could anybody from California want to hurt you for some reason?" Zane asked as they stood and started walking toward the house.

Caroline almost laughed. "No. My life was pretty dull. I worked for a company that owns a chain of Western clothing stores—nothing dangerous or dramatic about that. Between that and taking business classes at night, I didn't have time for much else. My business degree isn't finished but I'm close. I had good friends, all of them good people."

She didn't want to believe her little brother had been involved in anything shady, but that's where her thoughts kept circling back to. Could Owen have been living a life she knew nothing about? One that had gotten him killed?

Zane kept a close eye on everybody inside the wooden chalet-style building that served as the main office for Wilderness Photo Adventures. The property had been a family campground before Owen bought it. The building holding the dining facilities and even some tent-cabins were still standing, though they were shuttered up. He'd insisted on going to Caroline's meeting with her, even though

Matt had gone home and the police department had sent out a new officer to protect Caroline. Zane was here as a private citizen.

Sports celebrity Bobby Boom turned out to be a flashy guy with black hair gelled into spikes and bleached white at the tips. He was boisterous and obviously relished being the center of attention. He'd brought his own four-person entourage.

His social media assistant began snapping pictures of Bobby and Caroline on his phone as they stood and chatted in front of a window with a view of the deep blue waters of Lake Cobalt behind them. "These pics are beautiful," the assistant said as he moved around to capture different angles. "They're all going online right now."

Zane stepped in front of him. "Stop."

"It's cool," the assistant said, blinking in surprise as he lowered his phone. "I'll tag everything so it's connected to Ms. Marsh and her social media, too."

"Not the issue," Zane said in a tone that made Bobby stop talking with Caroline and turn to look at him.

The cop who'd taken over for Matt, a young guy named Steve Campbell, nodded. "We don't want anyone to know her location right now."

"Makes sense," Bobby said. According to Caroline, he'd heard about yesterday's attack on the local morning news. She'd offered him the chance to bow out of a business association with Wilderness Photo Adventures in light of current events. He'd turned her down, saying, "We can't give in to the haters, man."

Dottie, the office manager for Wilderness Photo Adventures, was also there for the meeting. The wall behind her desk was decorated with pictures of her six children. Zane figured being a mother to that many kids helped explain her response to what was going on around her. She'd given Caroline a warm welcome when they'd first arrived and offered to do anything she could to help. But right now she stood with her hands on her hips, looking at Bobby Boom's entourage lounging on the furniture and staring at their phone screens like she was itching to knock a few heads together. Zane got the impression she preferred a more businesslike atmosphere.

"Like I said earlier, I was shocked and saddened to hear about what happened to your brother," Bobby said, moving to pose in front of the office's river stone fireplace. "Go ahead and take some pics," he said to his social media guy. "We'll post them later." He turned his attention back to Caroline. "Do you think the same people who killed him are after you?"

She shook her head. "I have no idea."

Wow, what a sensitive guy. Zane clenched his jaw and reminded himself he wasn't here to lecture Mr. Boom on how to behave.

Caroline had warned him Bobby would be a little over-the-top. And that the meeting would be less about number crunching and more about Bobby "feeling the vibe." Still, Zane was getting annoyed. And suspicious. "You're based in Seattle, right?"

"That's where I live. My main store is there."

"How did you meet Owen?"

Bobby sighed. "He came to a demonstration on a new line of ice fishing equipment we were selling at my store. Nice kid, very energetic."

Something about his tone made Zane realize that Bobby Boom was about twice the age of the twenty-something persona he portrayed.

"Owen came back for some other events over the next couple of years. I thought his plan for a business to get people out in nature, get them appreciating the beauty, taking some good pictures, was cool. Plus, he had ideas to accommodate people with limited physical ability or mobility and I liked that, too. Add in that it was happening in the *booming* little town of Cobalt, Idaho, and I knew I wanted in."

He looked around the office with a thoughtful expression on his face, then finally clapped his hands together. "All right," he said as he spun around to face Caroline. "Book me for the dates in January that we talked about. Winter survival skills. We'll build snow igloos. We'll build emergency shelters with pine boughs. We'll have a great time and make sure everyone goes home with a bunch of awesome pictures."

Bobby turned his attention to his entourage who, as far as Zane could tell, weren't actually doing anything. Except for the social media guy who kept snapping pictures. "Let's go," Bobby said. He turned back to Caroline and shook hands with her. "I'm looking forward to working with you, so you be careful."

"I will."

They headed out the door and Dottie walked behind them, watching as they clambered into their rental cars and drove away. "That was interesting," she said dryly.

Zane stole a glance at Caroline. She was smiling and looking relieved.

"Here comes Vincent," Dottie said, still standing at the door.

"Vincent?" Zane asked. He glanced at Steve. The cop raised his eyebrows in response. They both headed for the door to take a look.

"Vincent Porter, he was Owen's business partner," Caroline said. "So I let him know about today's meeting."

Dottie made a soft snorting sound.

"But I thought he was working out of town this week," Caroline added.

Zane was confused. "Owen didn't own all of this? And that means you don't own all of it, either?" The front door was glass. Through it he could see a dusty blue pickup truck rattling up the drive.

"Owen owned most of it—but not all. He and Vincent were friends when they were kids," Caroline answered. "Somehow they got reconnected when Owen moved back up here. Vincent helped Owen do some repairs on the house when he first got it. Owen needed help getting this office up to code after he bought it, too. He didn't have much money to pay anybody so Vincent agreed to do it for a ten percent interest in the business."

"Is he involved in the day-to-day operations?"

Caroline shrugged. "I don't think he was

when Owen was alive, but it seems like he wants to change that now. He offered to buy the other ninety percent of the company from me after Owen died so I wouldn't have to move out of California. He said he thought he could get a bank to give him a loan for a reasonable price even though the business wasn't making much of a profit. But I decided to move back here and give it my best effort."

Zane watched as the truck parked and a man got out. Not very tall, but muscular and tanned. Wearing jeans, a white T-shirt and a weathered baseball cap. He looked like a guy who did physical work for a living. He jogged up the steps and into the building, casting a lingering glance at Zane and Steve in his police uniform before going straight to Caroline and taking both of her hands in his.

"I was working on a jobsite in Kennewick, but I started back as soon as I heard what happened to you. Are you okay?"

"I'm all right." She smiled at him, but the smile didn't reach her eyes.

"Is there anything I can do for you?"

"No. But thank you."

"Do you have any idea who it was, or why? Did it have something to do with what happened to Owen?"

Caroline shrugged and winced slightly. She

was starting to look pale and Zane wanted to tell the guy to back off.

He finally let go of her hands and glanced toward Steve. "I'm glad to see you have the police protecting you." Then he looked at Zane. He may have been Owen's friend from childhood, but Zane was certain he'd never met him before.

Caroline made the introductions. Vincent seemed to recognize his name—and didn't seem particularly happy to meet Zane. Maybe he was just a concerned guy looking out for his business partner's sister. Or maybe he had a more personal interest in Caroline.

"You just missed Bobby Boom," Caroline added.

"That's too bad. I told Tiffany to meet me here. When you first told me about your appointment with him I told Tiffany about it. She wanted to meet him. She watches him on TV."

"Tiffany?" Zane asked, wondering just how many people were going to show up at Wilderness Photo Adventures today.

"My wife." Vincent lifted his cap, rubbed his hand across his hair and then dropped the hat back down on his head. "She's going to be disappointed."

"You ready to go?" Zane asked Caroline.

She might be telling everyone she was fine, but he'd seen what she went through yesterday, and he doubted she had slept well last night. He could tell her strength was fading. It would be good for her to get back home and get some rest. And it would be safer.

Zane and Steve had checked out the main building where the meeting took place when they'd first arrived and made certain it was safe before they let Caroline go in. But there were other older and unused buildings on the property they hadn't checked out. And there was the pine forest that covered the surrounding one hundred acres that were also part of Owen's property. Someone could be lurking out there. With all the people coming and going and the associated distractions today, a gunman stood a pretty good chance of creeping up to the office and getting a clear shot at Caroline.

She had gathered up her purse, a satchel with her electronic notebook and a few other items when a silver sports car pulled to a stop just outside the office door. The driver climbed out, fluffed her dark brown hair and then started up the steps and walked into the lobby.

"Hi, honey," Vincent called out.

His wife gave him a fleeting smile as she walked over to Caroline to hug her, forcing Caroline to drop her purse and satchel into a chair so she could return Tiffany's embrace. Tiffany expressed her concern for Caroline and offered her help.

Caroline thanked her, and then Tiffany greeted her husband with a quick hug and kiss.

"It's so good to see you," Vincent said. "It feels like longer than two weeks since I've been home. You look beautiful as always."

She patted him on the shoulder. "Thank you."

Zane glanced around. He saw Dottie powering down her office computer and straightening things on her desk. He agreed with her. It was time to go. He walked over to Caroline and picked up her purse and satchel. "Ready to go whenever you are."

She smiled gratefully. Her shoulders were slumped and eyes looked a little swollen. Maybe she'd be able to sleep a little when she got home.

"All right, I'm out of here." Caroline gave a general wave good-bye to everybody and headed for the door with Zane and Steve beside her.

Outside, both men were on full alert, their

gazes constantly shifting and scanning their surroundings, until they had Caroline safely in the patrol car. Zane sat in the back seat beside her. He wouldn't feel any sense of relief until she was back home.

Steve checked in with dispatch and found out that Owen's SUV, which Caroline had been driving the previous day, had been brought from the office complex parking lot to the house. The officer who brought it was waiting there to ferry Zane back to his truck, still parked in that same parking lot.

Caroline turned to Zane as the patrol car pulled up into the driveway at the house. "You must be exhausted," she said. "It's been good seeing you. Truly. And thank you for everything. But it looks like your shift is finally over."

Zane watched from inside the patrol car while Steve walked her to the front door and she went inside. The click of the door closing sounded very…final.

Well, that was that. It was a good thing they hadn't given in to some kind of sentimental impulse. Agreed to stay in touch or anything foolish like that. Neither one of them wanted to relive the past. They both needed to move forward with their lives. If Caroline wanted him to stay out of her personal life, he would absolutely respect that.

But it wouldn't stop him from doing what he could to help catch the bad guys who'd tried to kill them both.

SIX

Zane flipped up the collar of his jean jacket. Then he picked up his coffee cup from the porch rail where he'd set it, wrapped both hands around the comforting warmth and lifted it to take a sip. He gazed up at the darkening indigo sky over the mountain peaks behind the Rocking Star Ranch.

"You drink too much of that coffee this late and you'll never get to sleep tonight," his uncle, Jack Henderson, warned as he settled a faded green corduroy barn coat over his broad shoulders.

"Oh, I'll sleep tonight. Don't you worry." By the time Zane had driven his truck back to the ranch earlier today he could barely keep his eyes open. He'd made it up to his room on the top floor of the old ranch house, kicked off his boots and then fallen face-first onto his bed.

The only reason he was awake now was because Aunt Rose got him out of bed by waving a plate of fried chicken and mashed potatoes with cream gravy near his nose. She'd told him she didn't want him sleeping all day, only to wake up and stomp around the house in the middle of the night and disturb her sleep.

She'd said it with a smile on her face. Plus she'd made his favorite dinner and favorite dessert. Once he was fully awake, he'd realized he was ravenous. And that he owed it to his aunt and uncle to finish filling them in on the details about what had happened at the lakeside office complex.

Dinner was finished, concluded with a big slab of huckleberry pie. Now Zane was stepping outside with his uncle to check on the buildings on the property. He wanted to take an inventory of what needed to be done before freezing weather set in. There were also a couple of chores left to be handled.

An unexpected cold front had barreled down into Idaho from Canada around noon, chasing away the earlier warmth. It just proved that despite the best technology you couldn't predict everything. Now, with the sun gone, it definitely felt like winter wasn't far away.

If Zane took a look now at what needed to be repaired, replaced or wrapped up for the season, he could make his plans tonight. Then he could buy supplies and get started on Monday. It would likely take about a week to get it all done. Maybe this planning would get his mind off of Caroline.

Tomorrow, Sunday, would include church. Time spent with family, including church family, meant a lot to him. And if past regrets started haunting him again, he'd be able to find someone to talk to. His congregation included men and women who'd served in the armed forces. They got together once in a while for coffee and to talk. Just to remind each other there were other people who understood what they'd been through. And all of them were available to talk anytime one of them started feeling isolated or just needed to be lifted up.

Zane's efforts when he'd first arrived at the ranch last year had been focused on infrastructure. Completing some repairs in the house. Rebuilding the stables and a couple of barns. Doing what he could on his own and hiring help when he needed it with tricky plumbing and electrical work.

Next spring they would start buying horse stock. Right now they just had the three horses Jack and Rose had owned for years. They were sweet-natured riding horses, but they weren't going to be producing any future generations of solid work horses.

Zane's long-time dream of living on a horse ranch was coming true. He was blessed, and he would be grateful and happy with that. His life was here and now, and it was a good life. Caroline was his past.

Several outside lights burned, but there was still plenty of ground between the buildings that was shrouded in darkness. "Forgot my flashlight. Be right back." Jack went back into the house.

One of Jack's ranch dogs, a speckled old hound with a sweet demeanor, meandered up and pressed her nose into Zane's hand, looking to be petted. As he scratched her head he couldn't help thinking of Millie and the little boy that dog obviously adored.

Owen's son, Dylan, was a cute kid. The spitting image of his dad. The kid shouldn't be forced to spend time with a mother who didn't want him. A woman who only wanted the money attached to him.

But that was none of Zane's business. He reminded himself yet again that Caroline had made it clear she didn't want him back in her life. So he would help protect her and catch the bad guys if he had the opportunity, but he would also stay out of her way and stay focused on his own life at the ranch.

"Now I'm ready." Jack reappeared on the wraparound porch with a yellow legal pad and a pen, along with the flashlight. "I don't know why we have to rush and check on all this tonight, but if you really want to do a walk-through that badly, it's okay by me." He handed the pen and paper to Zane and kept the flashlight.

They walked across the thick grass in front of the house to the gravel path Zane had put in as soon as he'd arrived and then toward the state-of-the-art stables he and Jack had recently finished after working on them for nearly a year.

"So, why exactly are you in such a hurry to do this tonight?" Jack asked.

"Maybe I'm inspired. Maybe seeing the business Owen Marsh started got me fired up."

Jack chuckled. "You've been fired up since before you even got here."

Jack and Rose knew all about Zane's past, including his broken engagement with Caroline, thanks to the email correspondence Rose had started while he was still overseas. Through the emails he'd also gotten reacquainted with the uncle he hadn't seen since he was a small boy.

Jack had gotten injured in a car accident a few years ago and needed one back surgery after another. He hadn't been able to do everything himself, as he'd intended, in order to develop the ranch property he'd bought as an investment and a place to retire, but at least he was finally on the mend. When Zane arrived for a visit the ranch was in obvious disrepair. He'd immediately gotten started with helping however he could. Then he'd bought into the ranch and put all of his energy into rebuilding it.

"How was it seeing Caroline again?" Jack finally asked.

Zane guessed he'd been dying to say something since Zane arrived at the ranch this morning. Rose probably had told him not to.

"Given the circumstances, I'd call it an emotional roller coaster."

"I'll bet."

Zane couldn't help smiling a little. "She seems to still have that strong will she always had."

Jack nodded. "Do you think her brother got involved in something he shouldn't have?" In a more gentle voice he added, "Do you think Caroline could have gotten dragged into it?

We all make mistakes. People can change over time. Not always for the better."

The beam of Jack's flashlight caught on eyes looking back at them. A doe. She froze. Jack turned the light away from her and she took a little leap before running off into the woods.

"I don't want to believe the worst of either of them," Zane said. "But it's crossed my mind. I thought about it when I was in the Wilderness Photo Adventures office today. Maybe there's a file in a computer, an image captured in a picture or even some physical thing tucked away in the office that could explain what's happening."

Maybe Owen had taken a trip into the back country and he'd witnessed something somebody wanted to keep secret. Or perhaps he'd uncovered something they'd wanted to keep buried. And maybe that person decided to permanently silence Owen and his sister to keep the truth from getting out.

Zane felt sick just considering the possibility.

Cobalt PD detectives were already hard at work on the case, but maybe Zane could do something they couldn't. He could try to find out if his dad still lived in Cobalt. If so, his old underworld connections might be a source of information. Maybe they'd tell Zane things they wouldn't tell the cops.

Lee had told Zane to leave him alone when he wrote to his dad in prison. But that was a couple of years ago, and he might have softened his stance since then. Zane was determined to help Caroline and her family. And there were questions of his own he wanted to ask his dad. Things he wouldn't have understood when he was younger.

When he had time, he'd start asking around in town and see what he could find out.

"Are you planning to see Caroline again?" Jack asked.

"If the police department wants me to help protect her, then of course I'll be there. Otherwise, no."

They stopped in front of the stable door. While Jack pulled it open, Zane glanced back at the golden lights spilling out of the windows of the ranch house. It looked warm and cozy, like home. And that's what he wanted. His own home. With his own family waiting for him at the end of every day.

Even if there was something intriguing about Caroline, pursuing that would be a waste of his time. She'd let him know that loud and clear. Besides, he'd worked hard to get his head on straight and learn to focus on the future instead of the past. He wasn't going to mess that up now.

The squeak of a floorboard sent Caroline sitting bolt upright in bed. Heart hammering in her chest, she tensed her muscles, ready to spring into action, and turned toward the source of the sound.

"Millie!" The dog lazily wagged her tail, padded the rest of the way into the room and rested her chin on the side of the bed, waiting to get her head patted.

Caroline blew out a sigh of relief and ran her fingers through her own tangled hair. If the dog was happy and relaxed, that meant her mom and Dylan were safe. For now. That was not a situation she could take for granted.

She rolled to the side of the bed and patted the dog, got out, stepped toward the window and moved the curtain slightly aside. The patrol car was still out there, but when the officer's shift ended at 8:00 a.m. that would be the end of twenty-four-hour police protection for the Marsh family.

It had been five days since the attack at the office complex, and everything had been quiet. No new attacks. No fresh leads. No proof of a connection with Owen's murder. The Cobalt chief of police himself had called last night. He'd been apologetic, explaining that they'd put as much extra effort and resources as they could into protecting the daughter of a fallen officer.

Starting today they would keep a patrol car in the neighborhood as much as possible, with frequent drive-bys. But that was all they could offer for protection. And that was probably why she'd been having one of those bad dreams about Owen when the dog walked in and woke her up. For several nights after her brother's body was found, she'd dreamed about Owen floating in water and calling out to her for help. That dream always made her feel helpless. And scared.

Enough.

She called the dog over to her where she stood by the window and gave her a few more pats on the head. Then she walked over and reached for her Bible, sitting in the bookcase shelf built into the bed's headboard. She sat on the edge of her bed and flipped the pages over to Psalms to read several familiar verses about David encouraging himself and shoring up his faith. She lingered over the words, thought about them and prayed.

Then she got up, squared her shoulders and put on her aqua-colored terry cloth bathrobe. She stepped into her slippers. It was chilly this morning. She headed down the hall to check on Dylan. Seeing him reminded her that there was still good in the world and that life goes on.

She and her mom gave Dylan the choice of where he wanted to sleep each night, and the last couple of nights he had chosen to sleep in his grandma's room. It was probably more peaceful there. Each day, Caroline had tried her best to hide her anxiety after the attack at the complex, but at night it all came back to her. Each night, her sleep was fitful and when she woke up the covers were tangled. No wonder her nephew didn't want to sleep in the same room with her.

She peeked into her mom's bedroom. Lauren opened her eyes and stretched out an arm, careful not to jar her grandson sleeping next to her. "Good morning, honey," she whispered. "How did you sleep?"

Caroline gave a slight shrug. At least her injured shoulder wasn't bothering her much anymore. "Sorry I woke you."

"I was already awake. And thinking about making a quiche for breakfast and brewing you some real coffee." Mom had to drink decaf. She claimed the smell of regular coffee, brewed for someone else, made hers taste better.

A short time later Caroline walked into the kitchen freshly showered, hair still damp, dressed in jeans and a long-sleeve T-shirt. Her mom was busy at the stove. Caroline grabbed a mug and filled it with drip coffee. She walked over to look out the window. The patrol car that had been in front of the house was gone. Caroline couldn't help feeling like they were on their own, though she knew that wasn't true.

"Mom, do you think we made a mistake coming here?"

Her mom put the quiche in the oven, closed the door and turned to her. "Where else would you want to be?"

"I don't know." Where she wanted to be was probably not so much a place as a time. Back in the past, when her father and brother were alive. When she felt safe. "I'm just thinking out loud."

It probably hadn't been smart to let her pride get in the way and goad her into telling Zane she didn't need his help. She hadn't been thinking. She should have known the police couldn't trail her every move for the rest of her life. Criminals knew how to bide their time and wait.

"I'm hungry." Dylan walked through the doorway of the kitchen with his favorite plastic toy, some kind of green robotic man, dangling from his hand.

Mom tightened the belt on her bathrobe. "Well, let's get you something to eat."

Dylan stumbled over and wrapped his arm around his grandmother's leg. She leaned down to kiss him.

"Morning, buddy. Can I have a kiss, too?" Caroline asked.

He walked over to her and she got down on her knees to give him a proper hug. She held him for a long time. Finally, she let him go.

Caroline had been amazed at her mother's emotional strength after two tragic deaths in the family and now the attack on Caroline. Mom leaned into her faith and that had helped her tremendously. Yet it was only recently that Caroline truly understood the stresses her mother had lived under for a long time. Living with the daily uncertainty of being a cop's wife while raising two kids couldn't have been easy.

The saying that you didn't really appreciate your parents until you became a parent yourself was true. Now that Caroline was a kind of parent to Dylan, she was much more aware of the sacrifices her parents had made over the years. And much more appreciative of them.

She would do everything she could to keep

Dylan safe. And her mom. If that meant moving back to California or somewhere else, she'd do that. If it meant swallowing her pride and asking Zane to personally help her look after her family, she would do that, too.

Her phone rang and she went to pick it up on the counter where it was charging. She looked at the screen. "Rowena Sauceda again," she said in response to her mom's questioning look.

The executive who managed operations at the Cobalt Resort was part of a committee looking to expand the resort's offerings. So far, the resort focused mainly on providing room accommodations and conference facilities, with a couple of bars, three restaurants, a few small shops and a day spa. Now they were looking into marketing "stay and play" packages that offered outdoor recreation arranged by the resort. At the moment they offered tennis, golf and activities on the lake accessed by the resort's limited dock facilities. Rowena had called Caroline weeks ago, offering to buy Owen's business. Wilderness Photo Adventures was located on a prime piece of property on the edge of Lake Cobalt. Owen had mentioned he'd gotten it at a good price because the family selling it had known their dad.

Caroline let the phone call roll to voice mail. "Well, selling the business and leaving town is an option," Caroline said to her mom, keeping her tone light in front of Dylan. Mom was aware of Ms. Sauceda's keen interest in acquiring the business, specifically to get its lake access with the nice sandy beach. Much of Lake Cobalt's shoreline was too rocky to develop.

Caroline thought the best decision would be to stay in Cobalt. The Marsh family still had a strong social network in town which would be good for Dylan. And for Caroline's mom. The beautiful mountain town was a good place for her nephew to grow up, and Caroline wanted to keep Dylan connected to the wilderness Owen had loved in hopes that it would help Dylan feel a bond with his late father.

Several of Owen's friends from the local nature conservation groups, along with some of his photographer friends, had offered to lead the tours at Wilderness Photo Adventures for the first few months until Caroline could get a handle on running things. Having these generous people around Dylan seemed like another way to help the young boy keep his memories of his father alive.

But what if she was wrong? What if staying wasn't the best decision?

"I know you're under a lot of pressure," her mom said. "But this might not be the best time to make a life-altering decision. For now, let's just have a nice breakfast and maybe you can get a little work done here at home on your computer."

By midafternoon Caroline's eyes were getting bleary as she sat at the kitchen table staring at the screen of her laptop. If she was going to stay on schedule and get Wilderness Photo Adventures back up and running in little over a month, she needed to get a lot done in a short amount of time. And she really needed to get back to the office to do some of it. Dottie was good with greeting customers and selling them photo adventure packages, but she couldn't take care of the financials.

Caroline looked away from the computer screen and out the window to rest her eyes for a minute. A vehicle pulled into the driveway, and she got out of her chair and grabbed at her phone so quickly that she knocked it to the floor.

"What's going on?" her mom called out.

"You and Dylan stay in the living room," Caroline answered in a shaky voice. And then, so Dylan wouldn't be frightened she added, "I'm coming in there to watch the rest of that movie with you guys in a minute."

Trying to stay out of sight while keeping her thumb poised over the phone in anticipation of dialing 9-1-1, Caroline hurried to a spot where she could take a look out the window.

A dark green pickup truck loaded with lumber and various other building supplies sat just a few feet from the door.

The cab door opened and a long leg wearing a cowboy boot stuck out, the heel resting on the driveway. Then she saw Zane sitting behind the steering wheel, talking on his phone.

Burning with fury, Caroline slid the locks on the front door, yanked it open and stormed out. "Do you have any idea how badly you scared me?" she hollered as she walked toward him. She didn't care that he was still on the phone.

He gave her a long look. "No, I can't say that I do." He said something into his phone, disconnected and climbed out of the truck.

His measured response made Caroline realize she looked and sounded like a mad woman. And even though she was still livid at being frightened by him, she knew it was a blessing that he was there. She had been planning to call him anyway—to swallow her anger and ask him for the favor of helping to look after her family. His coming before she had the chance to ask was more than she could have hoped for. She took a breath. That didn't calm her down so she took another. "Why didn't you call me before you drove up to the house like that?"

"You didn't know I was coming?"

"How would I know?" She threw up her hands. She knew she was overreacting, but now that her anger was fading she realized how scared she was.

"I'm sorry," Zane said. She could see in his eyes that he truly meant it. "I was in town getting some supplies when Matt called and asked if I'd pick you up and take you to the station to look at some more photos and answer a few more questions based on new leads. They want me to look at the pictures, too. He thought it would be a good idea for us to ride to the police station together."

She shook her head. "Why didn't Matt call me?"

Her phone started to chime and she looked at the screen. Matt. She took the call and disconnected a couple of minutes later.

Zane had been keeping his eyes on the street while she talked on the phone. Now he turned back to her. "Until I talked to Matt I didn't know that they'd taken away police coverage here at the house. Budget issues and any sign of police favoritism are real concerns.

But I know I can find people, some of them through my church, who would be happy to come out here and keep an eye on things on their own time."

Caroline took a deep breath and nodded. "Thank you." She wished all of this fear and anxiety would go away. That she could go back to being her old calm and balanced self. But wishing wouldn't make it so.

Facing everything head-on, starting with a trip to the police station, was the only way to get through this nightmare and get the bad guys locked up.

"Come into the house for a few minutes so my mom knows everything is okay," she said. "Then we'll go."

SEVEN

"That was disappointing," Caroline muttered as she and Zane pushed open the glass doors and walked out of Cobalt Police Department headquarters.

Zane scanned their surroundings, searching the road and sidewalk in front of the headquarters and the redbrick stores and coffee shop across the street, looking for anyone or anything that seemed out of place. Just because they were near a cop shop didn't mean someone wouldn't try something desperate.

"I'm not being critical of the police," she added.

"I understand," Zane said, realizing he'd been so focused on scanning the area he hadn't responded to her initial comment. "It's frustrating when you can't get a solution right away."

He glanced over at her and his gaze lingered a little too long. He couldn't help it. Despite all she'd been through, those dark brown eyes still held that hint of compassion that had always drawn him to her.

Caroline was smart. She always had been. By the time Zane was a teenager he had been skilled at turning on the charm to get whatever he wanted from people: Attention. Sympathy. Money. Somebody to do his homework. Caroline had never fallen for it. She had been too smart to be manipulated and she'd had too much confidence to fall for his flattery. He'd respected that.

But he'd fallen in love with her because of that compassion, that warm understanding that never felt like pity, just a quiet acknowledgment that life had handed him a lot of challenges, along with a calm, certain faith that he could overcome them. Make something of himself. Turn his potential toward something good, something worthwhile, rather than taking the easy way out. And as a result, he'd changed his behavior.

As he watched her look back at him while they walked, a strong breeze buffeted her dark blonde hair around her face. He thought about all she'd been through these last few weeks. She was handling her own challenges with remarkable grace and he was filled with respect for her.

"The police are working hard to develop leads on this case," Zane said, glancing away because he was a little worried that now, as in the past, she could tell what he was thinking and feeling. He headed toward Jack's green truck, parked alongside the curb with all the lumber stacked up in the back. "They said they were keeping Seattle police informed about any leads they developed, in case your attack has a connection to Owen's murder."

He opened the passenger-side door and she slid in. "I know they're doing a good job," she said before he closed the door. "I'd hoped we were coming down here for something more than looking at mug shots of unfamiliar faces, retelling the story of what happened to us at the office complex and me answering more questions about Owen."

"You never know what small piece of information might help an investigation," he said before shutting her door.

The sun had already dipped below the mountain peaks on the west side of the valley. Darkness was falling fast. Zane headed south out of town, following the main highway that ran along the edge of Lake Cobalt before veering into the thick forest for a few miles and continuing toward the area where Owen lived.

Had lived. Zane drew in a heavy breath. Losing someone you cared about was never easy. And the way Owen had passed seemed so wrong. Zane could only trust that the Lord would make it right. Trusting that He would take care of everything in His own time was the only way Zane could continue to shoulder the sorrows he'd carried since he'd served overseas and the sadness that had taken up residence in his heart even before he'd experienced the tragedies of combat. He had a few faint memories from his childhood when his dad was still a decent man. He hoped that Lee Coleman would be freed from his anger and addictions someday and that he would become a decent person once again. For the present, taking care of Caroline and the rest of the Marsh family was the only way Zane could do something for Owen. Leaving them without assigned police protection didn't seem right. He understood the explanation that it tied up valuable resources, was expensive and seemed unnecessary given that there was no sign the family was in imminent danger. But he still didn't like it. And he would do something about it.

Tonight he would park the truck outside Owen's house and keep watch. By tomorrow evening he would have several other people lined up to watch the house for the next few days.

"The resort wants to buy Wilderness Photo Adventures," Caroline said, sounding tired.

Zane looked over at the tall central tower of the Cobalt Resort, built on the lake's edge. Its glittering lights shone down and reflected off the rippling water below.

"I'm not surprised," he said. "It's been wildly successful. They're looking to expand."

"Maybe I should just sell everything and move us all back to California," she said as they drove away from the lake view and into the stretch of highway surrounded by forest.

Zane felt an anxious tightening in his gut at the suggestion she would leave, but he didn't say anything. She could make her own decisions. She hadn't asked his opinion. Their close relationship had ended years ago. Once the present danger passed, they wouldn't be seeing each other at all. Why would he care if she left? He didn't.

Except...

A wave of cold fear for her passed through him. "Are you assuming you would be safer if you moved back to California?" he asked. "Because that's not necessarily the case."

And if they were in California, he wouldn't be on hand to help.

A sound snagged Zane's attention. He turned to the passenger-side window just as something roared out of the darkness and smashed into them, bashing the truck bed behind Caroline and setting the pickup spinning as it careened across the four-lane highway.

Zane fought for control of the truck while his ears filled with the sounds of tires screeching, Caroline screaming and lumber falling out of the truck and slapping onto the asphalt.

It felt like it took forever for the spinning, sliding pickup to reach the soft earth on the road's shoulder where it finally came to a jolting stop.

"Are you all right?" Zane called out sharply, already reaching out toward her.

"I'm okay," she answered in a shaky voice.

The pickup had come to a stop with its front end facing the center of the road at an angle. In the glow of the headlights Zane could see a truck. It wasn't a semi, though it felt like one when it hit them. It was more like a heavy-duty oversized pickup truck, something for commercial use, with a heavy guard over the radiator. Maybe a tow truck.

It idled on the other side of the highway, diesel engine rumbling. Its headlights were turned off. Which was why Zane hadn't seen it coming before it hit them. And that told

Zane it wasn't just an accident. The driver of that truck had been waiting for them.

Caroline was already on her phone, frantically making the call to 9-1-1.

Zane took his foot off the brake, pressed down on the gas and tried to move his pickup forward. The engine growled and whined, but they weren't going anywhere.

Caroline had her phone on Speaker and he could hear the dispatcher say, "Officers are on the way."

Good to know, because they were sitting ducks.

While Caroline continued to answer the dispatcher's questions, Zane looked around, trying to figure out where the tow truck could have come from. His gaze lit on a likely spot, the point where a dirt logging road led out of the forest and directly onto the highway.

The tow truck's engine began to rumble even louder. In the glow cast by his own truck's headlights Zane watched the lumbering rig start to back up. The driver maneuvered until he'd eased his truck back up onto the logging road and was once again facing the highway.

"Staying in the pickup might not be such a good idea," Zane said slowly, a frightening realization forming in his mind.

"Why is he backing away into the woods like that?" Caroline asked, sounding puzzled. "That's weird."

Zane had a sour feeling in the pit of his stomach. "I think he's going to back up and ram us again. We need to get out. Now."

He quickly unbuckled his seatbelt and shoved open his door. He reached over, popped open the glove box and took out his pistol. He'd started carrying a weapon ever since the attack at the office complex. There was always the chance the bad guys would come after him for revenge or to eliminate him as a witness.

Caroline unfastened her seatbelt and he reached over to grab her arm and pull her out with him. His side of the pickup faced away from the attacking vehicle, hopefully giving them the chance to slip away into the thick forest without being seen.

The tow truck was still backing up, but then it made a shrieking sound as the driver slammed on his brakes. Maybe he saw they were trying to get away. The diesel's engine screamed as it lurched directly toward them, the driver turning on his headlights and flicking them to High Beam, blinding them as they tried to get out and scramble to safety.

Once they were free of the pickup, Zane shoved Caroline ahead of him.

The headlights bearing down on them grew even brighter. The screaming of the engine grew shriller. They were just at the edge of the highway where it met the woods when Zane heard the crash of impact as the heavily reinforced tow truck ploughed into the pickup.

Seconds later something hit him behind his right knee, knocking him to the ground and sending him tumbling down a slope just beyond the edge of the forest.

He heard other pieces of debris crashing into the trees and underbrush around him. Then the lights from the attacking truck suddenly went out and Zane was falling in the resulting darkness.

Finally, he came to a stop. The crashing sounds subsided and he could no longer hear the roar of the diesel.

"Caroline?" he called out, heart thundering in his chest and sick with fear that she'd been hurt.

She didn't answer.

He got to his feet, relieved to find that his knee wasn't badly injured, and called her name again. And again, he didn't hear her respond.

He was starting to get his night vision and

frantically looked around. Caroline had been beside him just a minute ago. Now she was gone.

The original gunman from the office complex had one arm wrapped around Caroline's shoulder and his hand clamped tight over her mouth. He held a pistol in the other hand and used it to shove pine branches aside as they headed deeper into the woods away from the highway.

Fear flooded Caroline's body, making her knees weak. Was he taking her deeper into the forest to execute her?

She gritted her teeth in anticipation of the blast that would end it all. *Help me, Lord. Please!*

The man was muttering, but she couldn't quite understand him.

"Caroline!"

Zane! Zane was coming after her!

"Caroline!" This time she could hear him getting closer.

She fought to wrench her jaw open and scream, but Handgun Guy clamped his hand down tighter over her mouth. She managed to get a small nip of his finger and bit down, hard.

He hissed in pain and cursed. "I can't wait

to finish you off." He tightened his grip over her mouth, digging his fingernails into her cheek.

Sirens wailed in the distance.

The man kept looking over his shoulder, obviously nervous. They moved through a gap between trees and stepped into the moonlight. She got a good view of his gun. This wasn't the pistol he'd had at the last attack. That weapon was probably at the bottom of a river or the lake, where it would never be found. This was a revolver without a silencer. If he shot her the sound would give away his location. It was probably the only reason she was still alive.

She stuck out her foot and tripped him, taking the risk that he wouldn't shoot her. But he took her down with him and kept a tight grip over her mouth, muffling her attempts to scream for Zane.

The wailing sirens came to a stop. She was disoriented and couldn't tell how far away she was from the highway. She didn't hear Zane calling for her anymore. Maybe the rescuers had gone in the wrong direction in the dark woods, away from her and her captor.

Her heart sank and her whole body began to tremble.

The guy roughly yanked her to her feet.

A few more stumbling steps and they were in another clearing. But this one was different. Some kind of service road. Overhead, she could see power lines.

Handgun Guy started moving down the service road, still dragging her with him and making better time now that nothing was in his way. They rounded a slight curve and in the moonlight she saw an SUV parked up ahead.

"Finally," her captor muttered.

Was his accomplice waiting inside? And what if that guy *did* have a silencer on his gun? Would he just go ahead and shoot her so they could make their getaway?

Caroline broke out in a cold sweat, waves of panic tightening her throat. She started breathing in labored gasps.

Handgun Guy kept looking around. He hesitated just outside the SUV. There was no one inside. He cursed, tucked his gun into his waistband and then yanked open the passenger door.

Illumination poured out from the SUV's dome light.

"Let her go!" Zane's voice came from out of the darkness.

Handgun Guy grabbed his revolver and

pointed it at the side of Caroline's head. "Let us leave or I'll kill her."

"We can't do that." This was a different voice speaking. Matt stepped from the forest to the edge of the light spilling out from the SUV. A couple of other cops appeared on either side of him. And then she saw Zane.

Still holding her tight, her captor pulled her a few steps away from the SUV. She prayed he would let her go and make a run for it.

"I *will* kill her if you don't back off," he shouted, shoving the tip of the gun into her temple so hard that it forced her to turn her head.

"We aren't going away," Matt called out, his voice sounding calmer. Caroline recognized that he was working to de-escalate the situation.

"Where do you think you're going to go?" Matt continued. "We've got you. Are you really going to murder somebody with a bunch of cops as witnesses?"

Caroline could feel her captor shift his weight from one foot to the other as he continued to hold her. Maybe he was going to let her go.

"Put down your weapon!" Matt commanded.

The man began to loosen his hold on her and pulled the gun barrel away from her temple.

Please, Lord, help him decide to let me go. Maybe she was going to be okay. Her mind raced despite her physical exhaustion. If this guy would surrender, the police could probably get him to talk in return for more lenient charges. Maybe he would give up the name of his partner. Say who hired them. Maybe she could find out who murdered her brother and why.

Her eyes were on the gun as the guy slowly lowered it to his side.

Crack! The report of a rifle shot made her flinch. The sound came from the darkness behind them, not in front of them where the cops were now taking cover behind the trees.

The bad guy fell forward beside her, blood covering the back of his head and neck.

She had no doubt he was dead.

Zane rushed forward and wrapped her in his arms. She clung tightly to him, both of their hearts beating so strongly that it felt like they were joined together. He pulled her down to the ground so they could take cover by the SUV. Caroline prayed whoever had fired that rifle blast wouldn't shoot again.

Thirty minutes later she was sitting in the back of an ambulance, watching as an EMT finished wrapping a bandage around an ice pack pressed to the back of Zane's knee.

A county sheriff's department helicopter flew overhead, its bright searchlight sweeping across the service road and the forest on either side of it. A K-9 officer and his barking, excited dog were searching the area, along with other cops, reserve officers and first responders, but so far there'd been no sign of the person who'd fired the shot in the darkness.

The back door of the ambulance was open and Matt walked up to it. "You still alive?" he leaned in and asked Zane.

Zane gave him a faint half smile. "Afraid so." His pant leg had been cut open by the EMT to assess his injuries. Zane pulled the jean fabric together the best he could over the bandage and ice pack and tucked the bottom into his boot.

"That was some good tracking on your part," Matt continued. "Finding Caroline in the dark woods like that."

Zane cocked an eyebrow. "It's why you pay me the big bucks in the reserves."

"Speaking of reserves," said Matt, turning his attention to Caroline, "the chief's moved a few things around in the budget and authorized the funding to hire reserve officers to watch your house."

"That should have been done from the beginning," Zane said.

Matt nodded. "Agreed. But hindsight is always much clearer, isn't it?"

"What have you found out about the guy who grabbed me?" Caroline asked. The man who was now dead. That was another image to add to her nightmares.

"We don't know anything about him yet. He wasn't carrying ID and the SUV was stolen, of course. His fingerprints have been scanned and sent but we don't have anything back so far." Somebody called to Matt and he stepped back from the ambulance doorway. "I'll keep you posted." He turned and walked away.

Caroline was sitting on a padded, narrow side bench in the ambulance. She wrapped her arms across her stomach and leaned forward, staring down at her feet. The feelings of terror and helplessness she'd felt earlier, when the gunman had her, were starting to return. She'd nearly been killed, *again*, and she still had no idea why. And she was starting to question whether she could handle the challenges in front of her.

Owen was gone. And it felt like she had a million impossible decisions to make to keep her nephew and mom safe. Maybe even happy, one day. Nothing was certain anymore. Hardly anything made sense.

I can't handle what You're giving me to do. It's too much.

"Hey," Zane said softly. "You ready to go home?"

She lifted her head, her hair fell away from her face and she looked him straight in the eye. "What if whoever wants me dead sends somebody to the house to kill me? What if Dylan gets hurt or sees me or my mom get attacked, maybe even killed?" Her voice was rising. She could hear the hint of hysteria, but she couldn't help it.

"Do you want to come back to the ranch with me?"

"I don't know." She shook her head and felt tears start to roll down her cheeks. "I don't want to leave Dylan and Mom on their own."

"Bring them to the ranch, too."

"But maybe that's exactly what would put them in danger." She impatiently wiped away the tears. "I need time to think things through." And time to pray.

"I understand."

"Now I have to go home and tell my mom I nearly got killed again." She shook her head. "I don't know how much of this her heart can take."

Zane stood up from the gurney where he'd been sitting, winced slightly and then held out his hand to her. "Come on. I'm sure one of these cops will give us a ride to the house. Let's make sure your mom sees you're okay before she hears about what happened. That might help ease the shock."

Caroline took his hand and stood up.

At least he respected her enough not to offer any false reassurances. That must be something they'd both learned during their years apart. Sometimes the worst thing you could imagine *did* happen.

EIGHT

The following evening Zane drove along the highway from Cobalt to Owen's house and used his hands-free device to call Caroline. The drive took him past the point where the tow truck had rammed them last night. When she didn't answer, his palms began to sweat. He couldn't help thinking about how close he'd come to losing Caroline and about the gunman who was still at large.

He left a voice mail message, asking her to call him back right away. Then he placed a call to the house phone. Mrs. Marsh picked it up on the third ring.

"Is everything all right?" he quickly asked, speaking over her greeting. "Is Caroline okay?"

"She's fine, honey."

"Are you sure? She didn't answer my call." Zane punched the accelerator a little harder. He was driving his own pickup out to Owen's house. Unfortunately, Jack's ranch truck was a total loss after last night's attack. At least Zane had been able to salvage some of the lumber and building supplies.

He'd seen Caroline safely home last night and hung around until the reserve officer assigned to watch the house had shown up. Then he'd gone home for some uneasy sleep.

He'd woken up several times in the night, heart pounding, after dreaming of Caroline hurt and him helpless to do anything. Finally, he'd gotten up and gone to work on his projects around the ranch. Temperatures had taken a significant dip and the early morning frost had gotten thicker. So he'd hammered plywood sheets over outbuilding windows, wrapped and insulated pipes and chopped and stacked some firewood.

The attacks on Caroline had started to bring up memories from his time fighting overseas. He'd learned a few coping mechanisms for stress and anxiety that worked for him. He kept busy. He tried to keep his focus on the here and now. And every time he started to worry, he turned his thoughts to Bible verses he'd memorized.

Late in the afternoon he'd gotten a call from Matt asking him to come down to the police station. The detectives working the case had a few questions for Zane about last night.

Plus, the police department had information related to the attack that they were willing to share with him and let him pass it along to Caroline. He was on his way right now from the police station to Owen's house. After her reaction to his arrival the previous day, he'd wanted to make sure he called and warned her before he arrived.

"Caroline's in the spare room where her brother stored all of the odds and ends he didn't know what to do with," Mrs. Marsh continued over the phone. "She's been making a big racket moving things around. Told me it was a mess to begin with so she couldn't make it any worse." She paused and Zane could hear her sigh. "She's talked herself into believing her brother had something somebody wants. Or something he wanted to make sure nobody found. And she thinks it could be in the house."

"What kind of thing?" Zane asked, intrigued. Had the guy who grabbed her last night said or asked something that led her to that conclusion?

"She said she was going to look through everything in the house, everything in Owen's computer here, and then she would search everything at the Wilderness Photo Adventures office. When I asked her what she was looking for, she said she didn't know but she thought she'd recognize something important when she saw it."

"I've just made the turn off the highway and I'll be at the house in a few minutes." Zane explained about the police releasing information and asking him to pass it to the family in person and in private. The details weren't something they wanted released to the general public just yet.

The connection went silent for several seconds and then he heard Mrs. Marsh sigh again.

"I'm so sorry," Zane said. Even though Mrs. Marsh had not been attacked directly, she'd suffered through several horrifying experiences with possibly more on the way. Experience had taught him that adding a lot of words to his expression of sympathy wouldn't help her. Doing everything he could to protect her family just might.

"Thank you." Her voice wasn't much more than a whisper. She disconnected the call.

When he arrived he took a couple of minutes to talk to the cop watching the place. Then he walked up to the front door and Mrs. Marsh opened it before he could knock. "Come on in." Dylan stood beside her wearing a gray-and-blue striped snowboarder's beanie tilted back on his head. It was way too big for him and had likely been his dad's.

The smell of simmering beef and spicy rice made his stomach rumble and reminded him he hadn't eaten since lunch about six hours ago.

"Hi," Dylan said, getting in the way as Zane tried to walk through the door.

"Hey," Zane replied, squatting down to Dylan's level once he was inside and Mrs. Marsh could shut the door. His injured knee hurt a little but it wasn't anything he couldn't ignore. "How are ya?" While the boy fumbled through his response—which included several words Zane couldn't understand, the phrase "You know what?" at least a dozen times and lots of repeating himself—Zane studied the kid's face. He hadn't had time to notice until now just how much the boy looked like Owen. And Caroline.

Zane stood up when he was fairly certain the kid was done talking to him. To his surprise, Dylan immediately tugged on his pant leg wanting more of his attention. He felt oddly flattered and smiled at the boy.

Having grown up without siblings, he hadn't been comfortable around little kids until a couple of years ago. Spending a lot of time at church meetings in the year after he got out of the army, he'd gotten a little more used to them. More than once he'd caught himself wondering what kind of a dad he'd make. He started to think about it now and shook off that train of thought. When it happened, *if* it ever did, it would be well into the future.

"Dinner will be a ready in a few minutes. Why don't you go tell Caroline what you learned from the police and you can tell me later." Mrs. Marsh gave a slight nod toward Dylan, indicating that she didn't want to talk about it in front of him. She grabbed some utensils out of a drawer and her grandson immediately became fixated on helping her set the table. Zane felt a little disappointed at no longer being the center of Dylan's attention. Apparently little kids were fickle.

He headed deeper into the house and made his way to a room where he could hear a fair amount of noise. Stepping through the doorway, he spotted Caroline sitting in a chair behind a paint-spattered old desk that was covered with open boxes. Papers were strewn everywhere. The closet doors were flung open and the shelves emptied.

A big mound of winter clothes sat on the floor next to a printer that looked like it had seen better days. Beside it was a plastic clothes hamper full of paperback fantasy novels and an assortment of sports magazines.

"Hey," Zane called out to get her attention.

She looked up at him and it felt like his heart stopped for a few beats. She was dressed in jeans and a sweater. At some point in the day she'd pinned up her dark blonde hair, but it had since come loose and strands of it stuck out in several directions.

When she focused the serious gaze of her dark brown eyes on him, all he could think about was how she had always seemed to understand things much better and more quickly than he ever had. How she had always known what was important and what really wasn't worth getting too worked up about.

Back when they were teenagers, fighting, angry, manipulative Zane Coleman had fallen in love with that girl so gently and easily that he couldn't possibly say when exactly it had happened. And it had changed his whole life.

But being in love with her was in the past, he reminded himself. And he had to let go of the past if he wanted to heal and move on with his life. And he wanted that very much.

"What are you doing here?" she snapped. There was a manila folder full of papers on the desk and she'd been sorting through it when he'd interrupted her.

"I called. Didn't you hear your phone?"

"I heard it." She glanced distractedly toward a phone resting on a windowsill. "I didn't answer it. I have things to do."

"I can see that," he said, stepping into the room and moving a few things so he could sit on the floor and rest his back against the wall. "I'm here because I have news from the police department."

Caroline's posture went rigid and she turned to him. "If Owen did anything wrong, I know he did it for Dylan." And then she burst into tears. She propped her elbows on the desk and dropped her face into her hands.

Zane started to get up and move to put his arms around her and comfort her. *No.* That was not a good idea. She might be okay with him doing that right now, but later the memory of it would make her uncomfortable. It would make it harder for them to work together if he did anything that seemed like he was trying to get closer to her.

He wondered if he should go get her mom.

"It's nothing like that," he said quietly. "It's not about Owen. It's about last night."

She leaned back, sniffed loudly and wiped her eyes. "Owen being involved in something bad is the only reason I can think of for everything that's happened." She took a deep breath and blew it out. "And I don't know what to do." She looked directly at him, her eyes red rimmed. "I prayed about it last night and again this morning. I still don't know what to do."

"So keep praying," he said. "Waiting for an answer isn't easy. I know that. But you're not trying to do the easy thing. You're trying to do the right thing."

She nodded. "Tell me your news."

"The man who grabbed you and was killed—we got a match on his prints. His name was Keith Young. He did have a criminal past, mostly robbery and assaults, centered around the Seattle area. The Seattle police department is sending detectives out to talk to his known associates. That's all they would tell me, but it gives them leads not only for the attacks on you but also potentially the attack on Owen. And, hopefully, that means they'll be able to bring whoever killed Owen to justice."

She nodded. "Well, it's still not the solution to everything that I'm hoping for, but it's something."

"After combing the area of the attack last night and this morning, the local cops are fairly certain they know what happened.

"The heavy tow truck was reported stolen over in Montana three days ago. It's likely

Young had it hidden on that logging road for a couple of days. There's some camping equipment and food wrappers up there. His partner must have been watching you. They assumed at some point you'd go past that spot, since there's no other way for you to get home from town. They'd also stolen the SUV and left it on the power line access road. The cops figure the plan was to grab you on the highway, get you in the SUV and take you out of the area."

She cleared her throat. "They probably wanted to kill me some place away from the valley here so my body would never be found. That way the police wouldn't be able to recover any forensic evidence. And they would likely waste time and resources looking for me instead of staying focused solely on the search for Owen's killer."

"Maybe." Zane took a steadying breath, not wanting to think about it. "So the one guy grabs you, and the partner shows up just at the same time that the cops arrive. When it looks like the guy who grabbed you might surrender, and possibly give information to the cops, the partner shoots and kills him. The partner might be the second gunman at the office complex. Nobody knows for sure. But he hasn't been found yet."

"You think he's still in this area?"

"I don't think it's wise to assume he's going to give up and go away."

"Thanks for dinner." Caroline wrapped an arm around her mom's shoulder for a hug. She'd been so wrapped up in the challenges life had been throwing at her lately that sometimes she forgot to let her mom know how much she appreciated all she did for her. "It was delicious."

Her mom reached up to press her warm hand against Caroline's cheek, then went back to folding the dish towel in her hands and draping it over the handle of the oven door.

"Your red peppers stuffed with beef and Spanish rice brought back some good memories," Zane said.

He stood a little ways away from them in the kitchen as they finished cleaning up, like he wasn't certain exactly how welcome he was.

The three of them had talked about Henry and Owen while they ate dinner. All happy memories. They'd actually relaxed enough to enjoy some good laughs. Dylan had thrown a few random comments in Zane's direction and seemed to have developed a fascination for him. Of course that was in between sliding out of his chair, running back and forth to the living room to grab toys and playing with his dog.

In the midst of it all, Zane had managed to get Caroline's mom caught up on what he'd learned at the police station without Dylan overhearing him.

Now Dylan looked wilted and was starting to whine. Lauren gave him an appraising look and tilted her head slightly. "I think this is a good time for me and Dylan to put on our jammies and watch a movie in bed."

Dylan gave Caroline a good-night kiss, then walked over to Zane and hugged his long legs. When Zane squatted down to get to eye level with the boy to return the hug, Dylan gave him a kiss on the cheek, as well.

As Zane stood up and watched the small boy walk away, there was an expression of longing on his face that took Caroline by surprise. Did Zane want a boy of his own? A family? She didn't remember talking about that when they were engaged. But back then they'd practically been kids themselves.

"Do you want some help going through the rest of the stuff in Owen's spare room?" Zane asked.

The truth was Caroline felt exhausted.

She'd been fueled by anxiety all day after a terrible night's sleep. She and her mom had already gone through everything in the rooms in the rest of the house. Once the spare room was finished, maybe she would finally be able to get some sleep. "Okay."

After an hour of both of them examining every scrap of paper in each box and file folder and looking inside everything else in the spare room, they'd found nothing.

"It's not like we can go into witness protection," Caroline said aloud after they'd been working in silence for a good while. "We're not eligible. I'm not testifying in a trial or anything like that."

Zane gave her a questioning look. Yeah, her comment was out of the blue. But all of her options and fears kept tumbling around in her head and she needed to talk to somebody about them.

"And if I move to another town, whoever is after me could track me there. Since I don't know why they're after me, I'll never know if I've left the danger behind." She shook her head. "The only thing I can do is stay and fight. And to do that, I need to have money coming in from Wilderness Photo Adventures. I'll work from home as I can, but there are some things I still need to go to the office to do."

"Your police protection can go there with you."

"I just hope having a cop around doesn't scare away customers. Maybe I can ask them to wear plain clothes and not bring a patrol car." She picked up a stack of photos to put back into a folder. On the top was a picture of Owen in a canoe, smiling broadly and looking happy and excited. Caroline felt her eyes start to sting with unshed tears.

Zane set aside the box of banking records he'd been looking through. Apparently Owen had liked printing out a lot of his documents. "I've been thinking about Owen's last visit to Seattle. He traveled there with his business partner, Vincent, right? Have you talked to him about what they did while they were there? Asked him his theories?"

"He said they went together for a meeting. And after the meeting they came back separately. I guess I didn't ask for a lot of detail. I didn't know what to ask, really. I figured the cops were taking care of it." She put the folder with the pictures in a drawer and closed it. "I never came up with any theories. I don't even know where to start."

"Would you be able to tell by his voice

if Vincent were lying, holding things back, scared, anything like that?"

She shrugged. "I don't know him that well. He was Owen's friend, not mine." Tension settled in her stomach. "You don't think he had anything to do with what happened to my brother, do you?"

"Maybe he knows something he's afraid to talk about. Some people aren't comfortable talking to the police. You could ask him a few questions, see what happens. Maybe he'd let down his guard with you."

Why not? She'd just told Zane all about how she was tired of being afraid, tired of having her family in danger and not knowing what to do. This was something she could do. And if nothing came of it…well, she'd be no worse off than she was now.

She took her phone off the windowsill and looked at the time. It wasn't an unreasonable hour to call someone. She put it on Speaker and tapped the listing for Vincent's name on the screen.

He answered after a couple of rings. She could hear a TV blaring in the background. "Hey, Caroline, I heard what happened. Man, I can't believe it. Are you all right?"

"I'm fine." She got the polite greetings out of the way as quickly as possible and then dove in. "Look, I've been thinking about that last trip you and Owen took to Seattle. Do you know where Owen was headed after that meeting you guys were at? Do you have any theories about what happened? Hunches? Anything?"

There was a long pause before Vincent answered. Caroline and Zane looked at each other.

"Like I've told the police a couple of times, I don't remember exactly where Owen said he was going after our meeting," Vincent said slowly. "We met with some people who wanted to pitch their business service offering helicopter tours during the busy winter tourist season through our office. We decided to shelve the idea until sometime in the future."

"And you two went your separate ways immediately after the meeting?"

"No. We had dinner. Talked about other ideas for the business. Then we parted ways. He mentioned Bobby Boom at some point. But Owen had a lot of friends in Seattle and there's plenty of fun things to do. I know he'd arranged for Dylan to spend the night with Dottie and her kids, so maybe he decided to go out and live it up a little. I didn't stay over there because I wanted to get home to my wife. Work keeps me away too much as it is. That's not good for a marriage."

Dottie had kept Dylan with her while Caroline caught the first flight that would get her to Idaho after she'd been notified of Owen's passing. She'd brought the boy back to California with her and taken care of him ever since.

"So you and Owen didn't drive over there together?"

"No, we flew."

"Vincent, do you have any theories on what happened to my brother? Maybe something you haven't mentioned to the police because you have no proof or you thought they wouldn't believe you?"

Another long pause. "I thought at the start that it was some random attack. A robbery. Something like that. But now after what's been happening to you, I don't know what to think."

"Yeah, I don't know what to think, either." Caroline thanked him for his time and disconnected.

"So what's your impression?" Zane asked her. "Is he lying? Holding anything back?"

"I don't know." She shook her head. "He didn't say anything odd. He sounded reasonable like he always does. But when I think about what's been happening, I can't help being suspicious of everybody."

NINE

Zane left Caroline's house and drove to the Bull Pine Tavern in downtown Cobalt. The old bar looked just like he remembered it. Fake split logs covering the outside of the building. Fake plaster snow slapped on the roof. Fake icicles hanging along the eaves that looked pretty grimy when you got up close to them.

He hadn't been by the place in years. It was located on a short side street that didn't lead anywhere he ever wanted to go. Back when he was a little kid his dad had dragged him there most nights of the week.

If Lee Coleman was back in town, someone at the Bull Pine would have seen him. It was his favorite kind of place. Dark, noisy and frequented by people who at most just wanted someone to chat with while they drank. Nobody was inclined to stick their nose into anybody else's business. If they did, they'd probably get it broken.

The inside of the bar also looked pretty much the same as it did years ago. Low lighting and bright neon beer signs. Loud country music blasting. The ATM at the end of the bar was new, though. So were the flat-screen TVs mounted near the ceiling in several corners, playing country music videos.

The old fake moose head still hung on the wall, with dusty blinking Christmas lights woven through its antlers. Those stayed up year-round.

When Zane was very young his dad would leave him sitting in a chair beneath the moose head where he'd curl up and fall asleep despite the loud music and people all around him. As long as he stayed in that chair and didn't bother anybody, the bar's owner didn't care. None of the patrons complained and nobody ever reported the situation to the police. When Zane turned eight his dad started leaving him home alone when he went out drinking.

Zane walked over to the bar, pulled out a bar stool, sat down and ordered a beer. He had no intention of drinking it, he was here to ask questions. Caroline's survival could depend on the answers he got. And if he wanted answers, he needed to blend in.

If there was any kind of scam or shakedown going on around Cobalt, Lee Coleman would likely know about it. There was a good chance if outside muscle came to town, particularly in the form of professional hitmen, he'd know about that, too. One of his many friends would know something. And if Zane couldn't get hold of his dad, or if Lee wasn't dialed in to the local criminal network anymore, he might try to track down some of his dad's old connections himself and see if they knew anything.

Zane took a deep breath and shifted his weight on the squeaky barstool. The police knew the kind of clientele the Bull Pine attracted and they might have already been here, trying to drum up a lead on the attacks on Caroline or even on her brother's murder.

But maybe Zane could scare up a useful tip where the career cops couldn't. He was here as a private citizen. And since most of his work with the police department reserves involved search and rescue, it was unlikely he'd had a run-in with any of the patrons here that would make them think of him as a cop.

He glanced around at the other patrons at the bar and the tables behind him, trying not to be too obvious. He didn't see his dad. But there was a whole other section around a corner where there were more tables and games. He'd check there, too, before he left.

While he was looking around he saw a handful of people drinking and laughing and appearing to have a good time. The rest sat alone with their attention fixed on the glass or bottle in front of them, looking as if they just wanted to disappear into it. That probably would have been him, too, if it hadn't been for Sergeant Henry busting his chops back when he was a clueless teenager and pushing him toward a better life. Certainly it was a much brighter path than the one that led to drinking your troubles away. That didn't work. Zane had tried it.

The first two years after he'd left Caroline and Cobalt were rough. He'd made some bad choices along the way but eventually he'd figured some things out. Now he was back home with the opportunity to build the kind of life he'd always wanted.

Caroline deserved that same opportunity. And he would do everything he could to protect her and stop the attacks against her so she could live out her dreams.

The bartender returned with Zane's beer and set it on the bar in front of him.

Zane pulled out his wallet to pay and asked, "Does Lee Coleman ever come around here?"

The bartender squinted at him with a face devoid of expression. He was a tired-looking middle-aged guy with a light brown beard. "Why are you asking?"

Zane gave a slight shrug. "I haven't seen him for a while. I'd like to catch up." Hearing his words spoken aloud, Zane was struck by how pitifully true they were. In spite of everything that had happened with his dad, including the fact that he'd made threats against Caroline, he still wanted to talk with Lee. There was still that tiny bit of hope his dad had changed. That they could have some kind of relationship.

"Who are you?" The bartender rested his hands on his hips.

The guy wasn't anxious to help, but at least he hadn't claimed he didn't know Lee. Zane reached for his wallet again, pulled out a twenty and tossed it on the bar. "I'm his son. Tell him I want to talk to him. Get me a pen and I'll write down my number."

The bartender shook his head. "It's not like I see him every day. Come back in a week. Bring another twenty and I might tell you what he said." He grabbed the twenty and put it in his pocket.

Zane nodded. It might just be a scam to get forty bucks, but it was something.

He stood up and walked toward the part of the bar that was out of view from where he'd been sitting. There were several people back there, but none of them was his dad. There was, however, one person who looked familiar. He sat a table with a couple of other men.

It took Zane a minute to figure out how he knew him. When he did, he walked over, pulled out a chair and sat down uninvited.

Bill Perry, the boyfriend of Owen's former wife, gave him a look that was curious but unafraid. His two companions didn't look scared exactly, but they looked concerned. Given the reputation of Perry, and the Bull Pine Tavern, there was no telling what kind of business deal Zane might have been interrupting.

Perry wore stylish clothes, had an expensive phone sitting on the table in front of him and would have looked more at home in one of the nicer lounges in the resort, hanging out with the beautiful people. Which pretty much confirmed to Zane that he was here conducting the kind of business that needed to stay under the radar.

One of his companions slid his hand under the table. Possibly reaching for a gun. Zane kept him in his line of sight, but mostly he focused his attention on Perry. Cold anger settled in the center of his chest. It was entirely possible this idiot was tied to the attempts on Caroline's life and to Owen's death. Perhaps he and Michelle planned to get Owen's money by getting rid of first Owen and then Caroline.

An oily smile slid across Perry's face, but the expression in his eyes remained hostile. "You were at Owen's house the other night. With the cop. Are you a cop?"

Zane didn't want to deny it, but if word got to his dad that he was associated with the police department in any way, Lee would have nothing to do with him. So he just ignored the question and asked one of his own. "Did you have anything to do with the attacks on Caroline Marsh?"

"No." Perry dropped the phony smile and shook his head. "I've got nothing against her. Nothing against any of that family."

"Well, your girlfriend's got a grudge."

Perry turned to his companions. "I need to talk to him for a few minutes. It won't take long."

The two men stood up and walked toward the bar. Perry sat up straighter in his chair and leaned forward so he could be heard without having to yell over the music. "Look, Michelle is my girlfriend. *For now.* When I get tired of her, which might be soon if she causes me much more trouble, I'll find somebody new." He laced his fingers together. "If she really does get custody of that little boy, it's over between us. I'd give her money to *not* take the kid."

"She's angry that she didn't get money from Owen's estate."

Perry shrugged. "How can I make it plainer to you? I don't care. She's entertainment for the moment. You know how it is."

Was Perry telling the truth? Zane wasn't sure. But he obviously wasn't getting any further information from the guy so he stood up, gave Perry a slight nod and then left.

Walking through the bar toward the exit, Zane's thoughts returned to his dad. He would likely be a more useful source of information. If he would talk to Zane.

Meanwhile Zane couldn't help worrying about Caroline. As the investigations into Owen's death and the attacks on her continued, whoever was behind it all was bound to feel threatened. They had to be caught before they lashed out again.

"I'm sorry to put you through all of this." Caroline propped the handle of a rake against the side of Owen's house and rubbed her hands together to knock off the dirt and bits of grass she'd picked up cleaning the yard. She looked into Zane's eyes. "If you haven't talked to your dad in years, it's probably for a reason. I don't want you to have to talk to him because of me if you don't want to."

"Don't apologize. You didn't start all of this trouble. And if he can come up with useful information it will be worth it." He rested his hand against the side of the house and leaned down toward her. "I'm helping you because I want to."

Caroline had been looking into his eyes, but now that he was closer she had to glance away. The compassion in his eyes made her heart beat a little faster. The way he'd been playing with Dylan for most of the afternoon had already set her mind wondering what he'd be like as a father and a husband. And now those hard-to-miss muscles under his long-sleeved T-shirt were just inches from her face. Gratitude, longing and affection were colliding in her heart and threatening to override her brain.

Zane had regained her trust. Absolutely. After years of thinking he'd never really cared for her and that he wasn't the decent human being she'd believed he was, she now knew he truly was one of the good guys.

But he had made it clear he didn't want to revisit the past. He wanted to move forward with his life. And she needed to keep moving forward, as well.

She already had plenty to keep her busy. First and foremost, she needed to stay alive. Then she needed to help raise a little boy. All while launching a business. She had no time for a relationship. Not that Zane was offering one.

Matt walked up to them. It was odd seeing him in civilian clothes with two little kids tagging along behind him. "Think it's about time to fire up the grill? Looks like we've got everything taken care of."

Caroline nodded. "Absolutely."

"Great." He headed over to the grill he'd brought from his own home.

They were in the backyard. Officers and other employees of the Cobalt police department, members of the church Owen had attended and some of Owen's friends had organized a work day to do some minor repairs to Owen's house and get the front and back yards cleaned up and ready for winter. Of course Zane was part of the work crew. And he'd insisted that Caroline stay in the backyard where he thought she was safer. In the front yard, she'd be vulnerable to anyone who wanted to drive by and take a shot at her.

Today was the first time she'd seen him in a week. He'd had work to do at the ranch. The police department had stationed a reserve officer outside the house 24-7 during that time. She'd missed Zane, but told herself it was just because he was someone with whom she could talk about her brother. When he stood close like this, though, that little story she told herself was hard to believe.

"I went back to the tavern before I came here," Zane continued. "But the bartender I talked to before had the day off. I'll try again tomorrow."

He hadn't told her ahead of time that he was going to try to track down his dad. And he hadn't told her about his trip to the Bull Pine Tavern and conversation with Bill Perry until just a few minutes ago. She wasn't certain why he was so hesitant to talk about it. Maybe he didn't want to get her hopes up that he'd be able to gather useful information from his dad. Or maybe it had nothing to do with her and everything to do with the painful relationship he'd had with his father.

She turned her gaze back to Zane. He wore a half smile as he watched Dylan and his dog race into the house with a new little friend, Matt's son, running along beside them.

She could see that Zane was a good and caring man. And yet…he'd left her. He'd let go of the connection he'd had with her family as if they'd never meant anything to him. Questions still lingered in the back of her mind. Was there some other reason for his leaving? She had to know for certain before she could completely let go of the past and build a new relationship with him.

"Tell me something," she said. He turned his attention back to her. They had a little bit of privacy while Matt and a couple of other cops were on the other side of the yard lighting the grill. "Were you being honest when you told me the only reason you left town all those years ago was because you believed my family wouldn't fight to help and protect you?"

"Yes." He crossed his arms and lifted his chin slightly. Maybe he didn't want to talk about it. Maybe he expected an argument.

"You really couldn't see how much we valued you?" How could that not have been obvious? She'd spent every spare moment with him. They'd planned their futures together. Her parents had issued him an open invitation to come to the house for dinner anytime he wanted to.

They'd been *engaged*.

"I know you have trouble understanding that but, yeah." He nodded. "You grew up in such a different way, with parents and a brother who loved you." He took a breath and let it out. His features hardened a little. "I could try to explain it using a million words, but you'd probably never understand."

"You're right." She couldn't understand, not really. But she could believe he was telling her the truth. And knowing he'd felt that way made her eyes start to burn and she quickly blinked away the unshed tears. Right now he was looking to her for understanding. Not something that looked like pity.

"But now I know I'm a child of God," he said. "And that I'm not worthless. I *really* know it, in a way that I didn't know it before." He took in a deep breath again and let it out. "Life experience finally helped me realize that."

The back door slid open and people walked out, some of them carrying tables and chairs to add to the patio furniture that was already outside. Zane gave Caroline a lingering look and then walked into the house and came back out a few seconds later carrying a couple of chairs. The evenings were cool this time of year, but they weren't too cold for a barbeque. Not just yet.

As the sun set and everyone dug into their hamburgers and barbequed chicken, she thought about how blessed she was to have the family she still had left. And to have these friends who were helping her and trying to keep her safe.

Determined not to get attached to Zane, she ate with a friendly trio of ladies from Owen's church. She'd just finished eating and happened to glance at Matt, sitting with his family on a blanket on the grass, when he reached into his pocket and pulled out his phone. He glanced at the screen and then looked directly at Caroline as he brought the phone up to his ear.

Fear turned the food she'd just eaten into a brick in her stomach. *Please, no.* Please let it not be yet another person she cared about dead or in trouble. Please let it not be some kind of threat that would put her friends and family in danger. A chill passed through her as he continued to look at her.

Her heart hammered at the base of her throat and she tried to tell herself it might be good news. Maybe the cops had a lead on whoever was behind Owen's death or the attempts on her life.

But when Matt got to his feet and headed toward her, she knew better. Zane, who'd apparently been watching from over on the other side of the yard while talking to his cop buddies, arrived at Caroline's side just as Matt did.

She set her plate on a side table and stood up from her chair. Her knees were shaking. "What is it?"

"Your former sister-in-law."

"Michelle?"

He nodded. "She's back. The man we have stationed at the front of the house intercepted her. She's demanding to speak to you. And she wants to see Dylan."

"She's doing this *again*?" So much for her hope that Michelle would give up on her attempt to get control of Dylan and his future inheritance.

She glanced over at her nephew. He sat on his grandmother's lap, resting his blond head against her shoulder. He looked sleepy. "Michelle's not going to see him tonight. That's for certain." She squared her shoulders. "I'll go talk to her."

Zane and Matt followed her to the front of the house where Michelle was pacing back and forth on the lawn. Was she drunk? High? Caroline couldn't tell.

"It's not enough that you keep my son from me, not to mention the money I should have inherited? Now you're trying to make the cops think I'm a killer, too?" Her voice sounded especially loud in the quiet evening. "They came by the house to talk to me a little over a week ago. My boyfriend wasn't thrilled about that. Then *your* boyfriend tracks him down to the Bull Pine Tavern and stirs up trouble there. Now he's saying he doesn't want the hassle from all of this. If he breaks up with me I'll be left high and dry and I'm not going to let that happen."

It looked like she was dressed to go out to the clubs, in a glittery deep blue dress and spike heels that kept sinking into the grass with every step she took, causing her to stumble. Finally she stopped pacing and stood still, fuming.

Zane, Matt and Jeff, the new reserve cop assigned to watch the house, had all positioned themselves so they could both keep an eye on Michelle and keep an eye on the street to watch out for any other threats to Caroline.

"Michelle, this isn't a good time."

"Why? Are you busy burning up the money I should have inherited? I see you're throwing a party."

"What do you want?"

"I want to see my son!"

Caroline shook her head. "Not now. Not when you're like this." For about the millionth time she wondered how Michelle and Owen could have ever been a couple. They'd skipped a formal wedding and gotten married at the courthouse three months after they'd met. Afterward, they'd taken a trip down to California. She had seen Michelle a few more times after that, but they hadn't talked much and Caroline had never felt like she really knew her.

Maybe someday if Michelle kicked all the substances she was addicted to, Caroline would agree for her to see Dylan. Closely supervised. If it was something Dylan wanted.

Until then, no.

Caroline shook her head and crossed her arms over her chest. "Michelle, you don't legally have any visitation rights at all with Dylan. Maybe that will change one day. But in the meantime, stop coming by this house uninvited. If you show up and cause a scene again, I'll look into taking out a restraining order against you."

Michelle's mouth twisted into an ugly sneer. "You'll regret that."

"No, I won't. If you ever sober up, if you ever get the chemicals out of your system and are capable of genuinely caring about Dylan, maybe we'll talk about you getting to see him. In the meantime, for Dylan's sake, I'll be praying for you."

"Ha!" Michelle made a scoffing sound.

"Don't embarrass yourself. I know you don't like me."

"I don't just pray for people I like."

Michelle stared at her for a few seconds, dumbfounded. Then she frowned. "Look at you, giving yourself one more reason to think you're better than me." She shook her head, then turned and stalked off toward a battered old sedan parked on the street. The boyfriend, Bill Perry, and his expensive truck were nowhere in sight.

"Let's get you inside." Zane stepped up beside Caroline. He was looking at the small stand of trees across the road as if he thought they might be hiding a sniper waiting to take a shot at her.

Caroline felt fear, sharp and icy, settle into the center of her chest. She was afraid of Dylan or her mom getting hurt. She was afraid for her own safety. She was afraid of running Owen's business into the ground. And she was afraid Michelle might somehow convince a judge to hand over custody of Dylan to her.

She walked with Zane into the house, feeling like she'd been living in fear for a very long time.

TEN

Millie's low growl woke Caroline from the best sleep she'd had in weeks. It was so deep and dreamless that her eyelids didn't seem to want to lift. She nearly fell back asleep.

Then Millie added a snarl to her growl and bumped her ear against Caroline's hand. An alarm went off in the back of Caroline's mind, sending her heart racing. This time her eyes flew open. *Dylan!* Where was Dylan? Was he okay?

Disoriented, she fumbled around trying to sit up in her bed, and then she realized she had actually fallen asleep on the sofa in the living room.

"Stay down," Zane called out in a loud whisper.

They had been watching a movie on TV in the living room. After the last of the friends who'd helped with the yard cleanup left, Caroline had been physically tired. But the un-

welcome visit from her former sister-in-law
had set her mind buzzing with anxiety and
she hadn't been able to calm it down. Worry
over the physical attacks on her, dread that
the danger could spill over and harm her family, fear that she really could lose custody of
Dylan—all had combined to leave her anxious and jittery.

She'd been determined to hide her increas-
ing concern from her mom and nephew and
the wonderful friends, old and new, who'd
come over to help. She'd smiled and tried to
dismiss Michelle's reappearance as something
she could easily deal with. But Zane had seen
through her act. After the last guest had left,
he'd asked for a second round of dessert. Caroline, her mom and Dylan had joined him in
the kitchen and had enjoyed a few extra bites
of coconut cream pie alongside him.

He'd mentioned a cup of coffee would taste
good and offered to brew it himself. While
sipping some from a mug, he'd suggested that
if he took tonight's guard of the house they
could all watch a little TV or chat a bit. He'd
sensed that companionship was exactly what
Caroline needed.

They'd all sat down in the living room,
picked out a silly movie suitable for Dylan to
watch and then Caroline, her mom and Zane

had talked. After Dylan fell asleep, her mom had said good night and carried him back to her room to put him to bed. Caroline and Zane had kept talking. Nothing heavy, nothing serious. Funny stories about Owen and her dad, mostly. High school memories. A little bit about what each of them had been doing for the last few years.

Slowly, her anxious thoughts had wound down. She must have fallen asleep. And now the dog had woken her up and Zane was urging her to take cover.

She heard the sound of scraping metal from the backyard area, like someone had bumped the patio furniture. Millie started barking furiously and lunged toward the sliding door, which was locked, trying to get her head under the closed curtain so she could see outside.

"Millie! No!" Caroline got up to grab the dog's collar and pull her away from the window, afraid whoever was out there might take a shot at Millie. The dog resisted being pulled away from protecting her home, and Caroline had to throw her full weight into wrestling the animal away to safety.

"Caroline! *Get down!*" Zane reached out and knocked a lamp off an end table, breaking the bulb and making himself and Caroline less visible targets to whoever was outside. Then he hurried over, grabbed Caroline and the dog and pulled them farther away from the sliding door and toward the center of the living room.

"Dylan! Mom!" Caroline's bleary confusion had worn off and now she was frantic to get to her family. Hanging on to Millie's collar as best she could while the dog continued barking and trying to lunge toward the window, Caroline bent over and headed for the hallway that led back to where her mom and nephew slept.

"Wait!" Zane commanded. In the low light, she saw him pressed against the wall beside the sliding door, a gun in his hand.

"I'm going to get my mom and Dylan."

He flicked on the patio light and she could see the clear outline of somebody holding a long gun. And maybe the shape of a second person, she couldn't be sure.

Then there was a loud blast and the sound of glass shattering into the room.

Caroline dove down behind the love seat, still keeping hold of the dog. She heard the sound of glass still falling, then the single shot of a handgun from inside the house. Zane was firing back.

Drawing in a shaky breath, she shoved herself to her knees. "Zane?" She was so terrified it came out as an exhalation of breath, so she tried again. "Zane!"

She peered around the end of the love seat and saw that he was okay. He'd moved the curtain aside a little and was looking out the window.

"You all right?" he asked without turning around.

"Yes." Help. They needed to call for help. Where was her phone?

"Honey?" Her mom came down the hall, keeping Dylan behind her. She held her phone to her ear. In the faint light Caroline could see her mother's eyes and knew she was terrified, but trying to remain calm for her grandson. "I've got 9-1-1 on the phone. Officers will be here any minute."

Her mom had been the wife of a cop for over twenty years. Not a life for the faint-hearted. Caroline suddenly realized just how tough her mother was. Even though she was physically frail, the woman still had backbone.

A second blast from the shotgun and the sound of shattering glass came from the back end of the house. The area where Mom and Dylan had been sleeping just a couple of minutes ago.

Her mother dove to the ground, covering her grandson's body with her own and dropping her phone. Caroline started crawling toward the phone to retrieve it when she felt someone grab hold of her arm and yank her to her feet.

"Kitchen!" Zane shoved her toward the opposite end of the house. Then he reached for her mom and Dylan to get them going in that direction, too. Millie was staying close by, no longer trying to attack the bad guys on her own.

"We can get out the front door," Caroline said.

"No," Zane answered. "They probably want us to panic and run outside. There's a good chance somebody's already waiting there. Better to hunker down and wait for the cops."

Caroline shivered at the thought that they might have bolted out the door and run directly into gunfire. Whoever was out there obviously hadn't realized Zane was in the house with them when they'd started their attack. They hadn't figured on someone being in the house who was armed and had combat experience. He'd parked his truck down at the far end of the street when all the volunteers had shown up and taken the parking places near the house.

Caroline pushed through the swinging door from the living room into the kitchen. They always left a small light burning in there and she immediately turned it off. There was one big window in the breakfast nook area that faced the street and another smaller one above the sink, both covered with blinds. Caroline watched her mom drop down to the floor with Dylan. The kitchen island was in front of them and the stove was at their backs.

Zane shoved a china cabinet in front of the big window. Then he hurried over and crouched down beside Mrs. Marsh. She had Dylan in her lap, her arms wrapped around him with his face toward her body. "What's the estimate for when the cops will get here?" he asked.

"I don't know. My phone's on the floor back in the hall." She kept her voice calm and steady while she stroked her grandson's hair.

Zane stood, snatched the house phone from the counter and tossed it to Caroline. She punched in 9-1-1 and was immediately connected to an operator who was well aware of the situation from her mom's previous call.

"The police are almost here," she said to Zane, relaying what the operator was telling her.

Suddenly a bright light shone through the cracks in the blinds above the sink. It looked like a powerful flashlight. Whoever was outside was trying to figure out where they were hiding inside the house.

They all looked at each other, no one saying a word.

Caroline did what she could to keep Millie quiet, but the anxious dog still whined and tried to bark.

The light vanished as suddenly as it had appeared. Caroline held her breath. Maybe whoever it was had given up. She slowly let out her breath.

And then she heard the sound of more glass crashing and breaking. It sounded as if someone were walking across the living room.

"They're inside the house," she whispered to the 9-1-1 operator, feeling the phone vibrate against her ear as her hand shook.

Zane turned so that he was facing the door to the living room and raised his pistol.

Caroline's mom continued softly talking to her grandson about going fishing and swimming as if nothing terrible was happening. While he obviously knew something was upsetting the grown-ups, he was also drawn into what his grandma was saying to him. Watching her mother and nephew sitting there and looking so vulnerable, Caroline was filled with terror and outrage.

She didn't have a gun. So she quietly grabbed

a heavy skillet out of a cabinet. Not a sophisticated weapon, but it was cast iron and hefty. She could swing it hard and do some damage if she had to.

The sound of crunching glass from the living room faded. Did that mean whoever was out there had gone to the other end of the house looking for them? Or did it mean they were about to burst through the door from the living room into the kitchen?

Caroline strained to listen. And then she realized she was hearing some kind of noise from the front of the house. Quietly to the operator she said, "I think somebody's at the front of the house now."

"Ma'am, the police are on scene. Where are you?"

"The kitchen." She quickly described the layout of the house.

"Stay there."

Suddenly exhausted, Caroline let Zane and her mom know the cops had arrived. Zane lowered his gun, but still kept his eyes on the door between the kitchen and living room. Her mom continued whispering to Dylan who appeared about to drift off to sleep.

Seconds later the police were in the living room, calling out for Caroline and her mom. Zane called back in answer to them.

Caroline blew out a shaky sigh of relief and thanked the 9-1-1 operator before disconnecting. Then she took a deep breath and closed her eyes. "Thank You, Lord."

She didn't know what she was going to do next. But she couldn't let something like this ever happen again.

Standing under the fluorescent lights in the police station break room, Zane watched Caroline reach over and lightly run her fingers across her nephew's ruffled hair. "I'll see you soon, buddy," she whispered softly, and then she leaned forward to give Dylan a gentle kiss on the cheek as he slept in his grandmother's arms.

Zane felt his heart rise up into his throat. He nearly choked on it when Caroline and her mom burst into tears as they hugged each other good-bye. Both women were likely wondering if they'd ever see each other again.

After the shooting at the house, the rest of the night felt like it had dragged on forever. The detectives already assigned to Caroline's case had been called in and Zane, Caroline and Lauren had given statements and answered seemingly endless questions.

There was the emotional aftermath of the attack to work through, as well. Though, sadly, both women had been through so much lately that it hadn't shaken them up as much as it might have otherwise. Dylan had mostly slept from the time the police arrived at the house. He obviously knew something bad had happened, but didn't understand the extent of it. Zane prayed with time the memory would fade.

Following it all was the unavoidable question—what should they do next?

Caroline had determined the answer was that she would stay as far away as possible from her mom and Dylan until she could be certain she was no longer bringing danger to them. And so now, at the police station, they would part ways for a while.

"Are you ready to go?" Rennie asked. Lauren's friend was there with her husband, a son and a son-in-law. She would be housing Dylan and his grandmother for now. Several members of Rennie's extended family lived on the property where her house was located, so there would be young kids for Dylan to play with along with the added protection.

Caroline tried hard to put up a brave front, but Zane could see parting ways from her family was a hard decision to make. Fearing for her life made her want to find solace in being with them. But she wanted to do what was safest for everyone.

Lauren sighed. Then she gave her daughter a watery smile. "Call me every five minutes."

Caroline managed a small laugh as she wiped away the tears.

"Millie, stay here," Caroline said to the dog as her mom, carrying Dylan, walked away.

Millie had started to follow them, but for the time being she would have to stay with Caroline. Rennie had a grandson living in her house who was allergic to dogs. There was no way Caroline would have Millie taken to a strange place where she'd have to stay tied up outside or shut in a barn.

The dog backed up a little toward Caroline, but then shifted her weight back and forth on her paws as if she wanted to chase after her boy.

"Millie, come here," Caroline called gently. Millie came to her, head dropped down sadly, and Caroline scratched her back between her shoulders.

Zane reached out to pet the dog, too, rubbing his finger over her silky ears.

They'd decided to part ways at the police station, rather than at Rennie's house, because Caroline didn't want the bad guys to know where her mom and Dylan were. She was worried that they might be following Caroline. So far the attackers were still at large. When Zane had looked out the sliding glass door, the one person he'd gotten a clear look at had been wearing a ski mask, so he couldn't give the police a description aside from height and general build.

Rennie's son was the last person to walk out of the break room. He paused and said to Caroline, "As soon as the police take down the crime scene tape and let us into the house, we'll collect some of your mom's and Dylan's things for them. Then we'll board up the broken windows and make sure the place is secure."

"Thank you." Caroline had dried her eyes and squared her shoulders. Zane wanted to take her into his arms so badly that he finally shoved his hands into his pockets to make sure he didn't act on impulse.

"I'm so sorry all this is happening to you," the son-in-law said.

Caroline nodded. "I appreciate that."

After they were gone, Zane turned to Caroline. He knew that she was hurting. That she was scared and tired and miserable. "Are you ready to head up to the ranch?"

"What I'm ready to do is leave town with Dylan and my mom. Get as far away from Cobalt, Idaho, as we can and never look back." She was staring at her feet.

"But you're not going to do that, right?" Zane's stomach muscles tightened. He understood she was venting her frustration. But he was also afraid she really would leave. And they had no way of knowing if running would solve her problems or leave her alone and defenseless when danger struck again. "You agreed to stay. And to move up to the ranch with me while Dylan and your mom stay with Rennie."

She nodded, but she wouldn't look him in the eye. And that worried him. He didn't think she was lying, but rather that she was still undecided in her heart about what she really wanted to do.

They walked out to his truck. Millie walked glumly beside them with her head and tail dropped.

"Well, I hope *this* truck doesn't get rammed by someone trying to kill me," Caroline muttered as she climbed inside and shut her door. She looked intently out her side window like she was scanning for potential attackers.

Zane couldn't tell if her comment was meant to be funny or not.

He didn't blame her for being afraid. He was afraid, too.

"Only a handful of people know where we're going right now. I think we're safe, but I'll be careful."

The sun was just clearing the peaks of the mountaintops to the east and there was a little bit of frost on the downtown roofs. Zane headed along the main street through town, which took him past the vicinity of the Bull Pine Tavern. In the next day or so, after Caroline was tucked up safely at the ranch, he'd need to make a return visit and track down that bartender he'd talked to. He still held on to the hope that he'd be able to talk to his dad, who might be able to tell him something about what was going on.

"I don't suppose any of your cop friends have given you more news about the guy who was shot and killed after he kidnapped me," Caroline said.

"They're *your* cop friends, too. They showed up at your house to do yard work and have a barbeque. That was for you."

She sighed. "I'm sorry. You're right. They're my friends, too." She dropped her head and then lifted it. "Good friends."

"Well, obviously the detectives aren't going to tell me much about an ongoing investigation," Zane said. "I don't know anything beyond what I've already told you. He had a

record and known association with an organized criminal group over in Seattle."

Caroline turned to face him. "Do you think
it's possible someone is trying to make it look
like the attacks are linked to Seattle when
maybe the person behind it all is over here?"

"I realize it's not much help for me to say
anything's possible, but right now that's what
I believe."

"I know the detectives are working as hard
as they can, but sometimes I can't sleep for
thinking about everything and trying to figure it all out. Why do the bad guys keep coming after *me*?"

She shook her head as if clearing her
thoughts. "I've looked at the texts and photos
and emails Owen sent me over the last few
months before he died, wondering if there's
something there that would explain it all. The
only idea that makes any sense to me is that
someone believes I have something or know
something and that's a problem for them. But
I can't see how anything Owen said or sent to
me could be the cause for all of this."

Millie had settled on the floorboard by Caroline's feet with her chin resting on Caroline's
knee. Caroline patted her head, trying to reassure the dog who obviously missed her boy.

They were on the highway now, headed

north, away from Owen's house. The highway at this end of town quickly rose in elevation, weaving back and forth along the mountainside. Slanted early morning sunlight flickered between the trees. Towering peaks, looking bluish in the morning light, rose in the distance.

"I know it's impossible for you not to think about everything," Zane said. "But maybe at the ranch you'll be able to let your mind slow down a little bit so you can catch up on your sleep."

"That would be nice," she said glumly.

"The more time I spend in nature, the more I'm reminded there is a God in control of everything. Even if I don't understand what He's doing."

She brushed the hair out of her face. "The way you stay so calm and cool most of the time makes it easy for me to forget that you've been through a lot, too. And I probably don't say thank you enough."

He glanced over at her sad, exhausted face and wished he could solve everything for her, say something that would make her feel better. But pretty words weren't what she needed right now. "You do what you have to. You put one foot in front of the other. And you trust God as much as you possibly can."

"I think I can do that," Caroline whispered.

A few minutes later they were at the turnoff for the Rocking Star Ranch. Zane followed a dirt road between a couple of hilltops until it dropped down into a small valley with thick grass, tall trees, a ranch house, stables and barns. This was his home now. And just the sight of it made him feel more peaceful.

Beside him, Caroline sat up a little straighter. "This place is beautiful."

"Maybe you can get some rest here," he said. He would need to catch up on his rest, too. Last night the bad guys had come dangerously close to their goal of killing Caroline. Zane had no doubt they'd try again. And he had to be ready to stop them.

ELEVEN

"A person shouldn't need a degree in engineering to make a cup of coffee," Caroline muttered as she stood in the Rocking Star Ranch kitchen fumbling with the contraption sitting atop the blue-and-white flecked counter top. There was a clear container of whole beans attached to the top of the coffeepot and she *needed* a cup of coffee to figure out how to get the beans ground and into the filter. And after that where did she add the water?

She glanced at Millie, lying on a throw rug beside a side door, her only company in the kitchen at the moment. Millie kept her chin on her front paws but raised her ears and then let them drop down.

"You're right. Maybe I'll just have tea." She'd opened and closed a couple of cabinets looking for tea bags when she heard the swinging door from the dining room open and turned to see Zane's Aunt Rose walking in cinching the belt on her powder blue flannel bathrobe.

Millie's tail wagged slowly.

"Good morning." She offered Caroline a friendly grin and reached down to scratch the dog on the head. "What can I help you find?"

Caroline cringed inwardly. She must have made a bigger racket than she'd realized. "I'm sorry I woke you."

It was so early the sun wasn't even up yet. After arriving at the ranch yesterday morning she'd met Rose and Jack, gotten a tour of the place and then tried to take a nap. She'd dreamt about the attack at Owen's house and her sleep had been fitful. She'd been served a dinner that was probably delicious but Caroline had been too stressed to be interested in her food. The bad dreams returned and she awoke every hour. Finally she just got out of bed and went in search of coffee.

"You didn't wake me. I'm an early bird. Jack used to be one, too." She pressed her lips together. "Until he got old and lazy." She grinned and her gray eyes held a glint of mischief. Then her gaze shifted to the mug Caroline had set on the counter.

"I can't figure out your coffee machine," Caroline confessed.

"Jack can't either. He says that's why I got

it, to torment him, but that's not true. I just like new contraptions."

A short time later Caroline was sitting at the small breakfast table pushed up against a kitchen wall, sipping coffee made from freshly ground beans and thinking she needed to get a coffeemaker like Rose's.

Rose had set about mixing some kind of batter, without a recipe, Caroline noted. After pouring the batter into muffin tins and topping each with brown sugar, chopped nuts and some melted butter, Rose popped the tins in the oven. Then she poured herself some coffee and sat down at the table across from Caroline.

"So, you're the girl Zane was engaged to," Rose said.

Caroline felt a twinge in her stomach. "He told you about that?"

Rose nodded. She rubbed her finger up and down the side of her coffee cup a few times before finally saying, "I should my mind my own business, but I don't want to."

Caroline didn't want to be rude to the woman who'd invited her into her home. But her past relationship with Zane was a tender subject with her. Plus, she didn't understand her feelings about him right now and it wasn't a topic she could talk about casually. If Rose had a specific question in mind she needed to just ask it. "It was a long time ago," she finally said.

Rose looked her directly in the eyes. "What about now?"

Caroline's cheeks started to burn. She didn't appreciate being put on the spot, especially by a woman she'd only just met. Even if that woman was helping her to hide from people who were trying to kill her.

But then hadn't Caroline told more than one person that she prided herself on being direct? And Rose wasn't asking in a rude or demanding way. Not really. And she didn't seem gossipy. She seemed concerned.

"He brought you home," Rose said when Caroline didn't respond. "That tells me he cares about you."

"He likes to help people," Caroline said softly.

"Yeah." Rose nodded her head. "But he doesn't bring them home."

Caroline let her gaze drift down to the tabletop, where she rubbed away a drop of coffee she'd spilled. She'd let herself become attracted to Zane. Maybe she'd let it show even though she hadn't meant to. It felt good to be around him again. To let him take care of her a little. To be near him. Even knowing she couldn't possibly start a romantic relationship right now. Even after he'd *told* her the past was past and he wanted to leave it there.

He was a tough man. But he was also human. He had vulnerabilities, too. Maybe he was lonely. Lots of people went against their better judgment when they were lonely. And it could be that hoping for a connection with someone was making him invest more emotion in her than he'd intended to. Maybe it was Caroline's turn to be strong. Make it clear they had no future together.

"I'm sorry I upset you," Rose said. She reached over and placed her hand atop Caroline's. "I have nothing against you, at all. It's just that Zane's been through a lot."

"I know," Caroline said quietly. "Until he left town, I was there with him. I know his childhood was rough. He hasn't talked a lot about his military service, but obviously that couldn't have been easy, either."

Rose tapped her fingers on the tabletop. "His uncle and I should have been there for him when he was young, too. Zane's mom and Jack were half-siblings. There was a very big difference in their ages, and the family wasn't really close. Jack and I moved to Colorado right after we got married." Rose took a sip of coffee. "Anyway, when we found out Lee had been sent to prison, I started looking for Zane. That's when I tracked him down to the army and, with the help of the USO, sent the email that got us connected."

Caroline nodded, glad someone was looking after him. Not that he ever thought he needed looking after.

The oven timer chimed and Rose got up to take her muffins out of the oven.

The swinging door opened and Zane strode in. "Good morning."

While Caroline and Rose returned his greeting, Millie got to her feet and padded toward him. He patted her head, then glanced at the pan Rose had set on the stove top to cool. "That smells good. And coffee's ready, too." He grabbed a mug, filled it, then turned and leaned back against the counter. He nodded at Caroline. "How'd you sleep?"

Despite having just convinced herself she needed to reestablish the emotional distance between them, a flutter of excitement had risen in the center of Caroline's chest the moment she saw him. It didn't matter that he still needed to shave or that he had a couple of sleep creases on his cheek.

"I didn't sleep much at all," she mumbled in answer to his question. She resisted the temptation to smooth down her hair. She knew it was frizzy. She'd seen the dark circles under her eyes in the bathroom mirror before she came downstairs and had almost frightened herself. Maybe looking terrible this morning was a blessing. Maybe it would dampen his interest in her and get them back on more of a "just friends" footing.

She was surprised when she realized what she was thinking. Did she really want to be friends with him?

Zane took a sip of coffee. "Why don't you get dressed and you can help me with some chores. Then we can come back and eat." Through the window behind him she could see the sky had shifted from black to deep blue.

She got to her feet. "I need to take a shower first."

He laughed. It was a quick sound of delight that made her smile in return. "We're going to muck out some stalls, feed some animals and clean out a couple of watering troughs," he said. "You're going to want to shower *after* that."

She let her glance slide toward the fresh baked muffins. "Can't we eat first?"

He set his empty coffee mug on the counter. "We'll get the chores done first. Then breakfast, then back to work."

She nodded. "All right."

"If you do hard, physical work during the day, you sleep better at night," he said. "It works for me."

Later that week, Zane was surprised to see how chipper Caroline looked so early in the morning. But after five days working at the ranch, she was finally feeling better and getting some sound sleep. At least that's what she'd reported.

The day after he'd brought her to the ranch, he'd gone back into Cobalt to meet Mrs. Marsh and Rennie's sons at Owen's house. He'd returned with the clothes for Caroline that her mother had packed in a couple of suitcases plus the laptop Caroline had asked for.

Since then, despite a multitude of conversations with her nephew and her mother on the phone and via the computer, she was still anxious to see them in person and convince herself they were well. And Dylan had started getting weepy over missing his dog.

Aware of the importance of morale when healing both physically and mentally, Zane had finally agreed they should be able to meet.

So he, Caroline and Millie were leaving the ranch and heading down to Rennie's home in Cobalt while it was still dark. Caroline stood in the kitchen pouring herself a travel mug of coffee. She snapped the lid on it and turned to Zane. "Okay, let's go."

With Millie at Caroline's heels, they headed to Rose's SUV rather than Zane's truck. Jack would follow them to the end of the drive in the battered old station wagon he was driving until he bought a replacement truck. He'd hang back to see if they were followed after they turned out onto the highway. If it looked like they'd made a clean getaway, Jack would follow them into town and park at the end of Rennie's street where he could keep an eye on things while they were at her house.

"Millie, lay down." Caroline gently tried to get the dog calmed and settled on the floorboard by her feet. It was apparently the animal's favorite place when traveling. And like everybody else, Millie's nerves seemed a bit on edge.

"We need to be quiet when we get there," Caroline said to Zane. "I don't want to wake Dylan. I just want to be there when he gets up."

It's not going to be easy keeping Millie quiet when she realizes she's in the same house as *Dylan.* Zane smiled to himself and nodded. "Understood."

Zane was anxious for life back to get

back to normal for the little boy. He'd been through so much and deserved a settled life surrounded by his aunt, his grandmother and his beloved dog. Wanting to do everything he could to help the Marsh family, including finding out any information he could share with them, Zane had visited the Cobalt police station yesterday. He'd learned that, after the attack at Owen's house, the Seattle police department had ramped up the pressure on members of the criminal group on the coast who appeared to be tied to Caroline's kidnapper and possibly Owen's murderer. Locally, the Cobalt police were checking with informants and still processing the bullets, shell casings, footprints and other physical evidence left at Owen's house after the latest attack. Whatever information they may have uncovered they understandably held close to their chest. But at least Zane had something to report back to Caroline to show her people were working hard to help her even if she couldn't see their actions.

After he'd left the police department he'd gone by the Bull Pine Tavern. This time the bartender he'd spoken to previously was there. He told Zane that Lee Coleman knew his son was looking for him. When Zane had asked if his dad was willing to talk to him, the bartender had shrugged. After Zane gave him twenty bucks, the guy had shrugged again and said, "Check back with me in a few days."

Zane hadn't been surprised. He knew his dad was a suspicious man who liked to lurk in the shadows.

"So is my dad here, in Cobalt?" Zane had asked.

Again, he'd gotten a shrug in response. He'd just have to wait.

Now, driving down the mountainside toward Cobalt, there was very little traffic on the highway. Which was good. It would make it easier to see if they were being followed. They reached the outskirts of Cobalt and then passed through the center of town where most of the businesses were still closed.

"You don't think anyone at the resort would want Owen's property badly enough to kill me, do you?" Caroline asked.

Zane followed her gaze and glanced over at the lake. The stretch they were passing through offered a beautiful view of the resort tower with its golden lights shining bright in the darkness.

"It's hard to believe they would. But I'm often surprised by what people will do for money." Considering how he'd grown up, it was a wonder he didn't always believe the worst about people. "They've done so well so quickly. I'm sure the owners regret not buying more lakeside property when they got started.

"But I can't see why anyone would assume Owen's land would automatically go up for sale if something happened to you."

"I've thought about that, as well," Caroline said. "Maybe it's common for heirs of a small business to cash everything out if the owner dies. If something happened to me, I can't see Mom running the day-to-day operations of Owen's business. But she could hire someone to do it. And I think she'd try to keep it going rather than sell it." She took in a deep breath of air and blew it out. "Now is probably as good a time as any to tell you I need to go into the Wilderness Photo Adventures office and do some work."

Zane gripped the steering wheel a little tighter. "I thought after this visit today you'd stay out of sight up at the ranch for a while."

"I'd like to do that. Believe me. I've taken care of as much as I can online to get us ready to open for business. But there are still a few things I need to take care of at the office."

Zane started to object and she held up her hand. "I'm not going to do anything foolish," she continued. "We don't have to go there today. But we're down to just a month before our official opening and that *has* to go well."

From the corner of his eye Zane saw her cross her arms over her chest.

"And I want to search the office and make sure there isn't something hidden somewhere. Something somebody want's bad enough to kill me for it."

Zane ran his hand over his chin. "That's a big piece of property. And there are several buildings on it besides the office. All the old buildings from when it used to be a camp-ground. If there's something hidden there, it could be anywhere. And if anyone is watching while you go out looking around in the storage sheds and the boathouse and the other buildings, you'll be making yourself an easy target."

"You're right." She uncrossed her arms and turned to him. "Will you help me look?"

He couldn't keep her from doing what she thought she had to do. And he didn't want her searching the property without him. "Of course."

Rennie's home was a small farm located at the end of a short dead-end road. When they arrived, Zane kept his eye on his rear-view mirror until he saw Jack's station wagon turn onto the road behind them and park. Seconds later, Zane's phone chimed with a text from his uncle, confirming he was in place and ready to keep an eye on things while Caroline and her family enjoyed a nice visit.

Rennie met them in front of the sprawling white wood-frame house and had them bring Millie into the sunroom in the back. Rennie's dog-allergic grandson rarely went into the sunroom, and its tile floor and simple furniture would be easy to clean after they left. Caroline had just sat down on a sofa when her mom walked in. Millie barked with joy at the sight of her.

Zane watched Mrs. Marsh wrap her daughter in a tight hug and hold on for a long time. Millie managed to excitedly push her way between them until she was standing on their feet.

Rennie and her daughter came in with a coffeepot, cups and a basket of sliced strawberry bread. Her son-in-law tried to get Zane to sit down, but he felt better standing. This visit was as secure as he could make it, but he wanted to be ready to respond quickly should anything happen. And he very much hoped he wouldn't need the gun tucked under his jacket.

Caroline and her mom ended their teary-eyed embrace. Before sitting down, Mrs. Marsh patted her grandson's beloved dog on the head. In response, Millie gave another joyful bark, followed by a guilty lowering of her head and a remorseful wag of her tail when Caroline shushed her.

Drawn in by the high emotion of the moment, Zane thought about how much he wanted a family of his own. He would always be a friend to the Marsh family. But standing on the sidelines of a happy family was not enough for him anymore. He realized that now. Maybe he hadn't found a wife yet because he hadn't been ready. He was ready now.

"Millie!" a young boy's voice called out. The dog yelped and sprinted for the doorway as Dylan appeared, his eyes still sleep swollen and a huge grin on his face. He ended up shoved against the door jamb, giggling, while Millie jumped up on him and gave his chin and cheeks several good licks.

Mrs. Marsh calmed the dog and got her to lay down so Caroline could swoop up her nephew for a hug.

Zane was surprised to find himself wanting to hug the kid, too. He'd missed seeing the boy over the last week. Dylan really was a sweet little guy. Cute. And he had his father's friendly nature. Zane was suddenly flooded with a fierce desire to protect the kid. And not only from the people who were trying to kill the boy's aunt.

As long as Michelle and whatever boyfriend she had at the moment were lurking around, trying to use the boy to get money, Dylan would need somebody to look out for him. Zane would be more than happy to take on that job. And maybe a little more, too. The boy would need somebody to teach him how to throw a ball, how to fish, how to ride a bike. Zane realized he would like to be that person.

When Dylan let go of Caroline and smiled at Zane, he felt like giving the kid anything he wanted just to keep him smiling like that. No wonder so many kids ended up spoiled.

Dylan started toward him and he knelt down so the boy could give him a good strong hug.

He felt an odd sense of disappointment when Dylan let go of him and he straightened back up. There was a selfish part of Zane that wanted to protect his heart from getting too attached. Despite his strong sense of loyalty, he had sometimes thought about walking away from the Marsh family after all the attacks against Caroline stopped. Just to keep his heart safe.

He realized now that he would never be able to do that. No matter what the future held, his connection with the Marshes would always have a place in his heart. Even if that opened him up to the chance of pain, it was worth it.

But as much as he wanted to envision a good future for Caroline's family and for himself, he still had to keep his attention focused on the present. Caroline was in danger. If the bad guys got desperate enough, they might use Mrs. Marsh or Dylan to get to Caroline.

Right now, it was Zane's job was to keep them all safe.

TWELVE

"I don't know how wise it was of you to come down here," Vincent said to Caroline.

It had been a couple of days since her visit with Dylan and her mom, and Caroline was finally able to somewhat set her focus back on her brother's business.

She glanced up at Vincent from her desk at Wilderness Photo Adventures. The fine lines in the face of her brother's business partner had deepened since she'd first arrived in Cobalt after Owen's death. She knew he worked hard in the construction trade and often had to travel to get work. Maybe someday the ten percent interest he owned in Wilderness Photo Adventures would really be worth something, freeing him up to take fewer jobs. She hoped so. "I have to get this place up and running on time to meet the financial commitments I've made. Otherwise, it all collapses."

Vincent shoved his hands into his pockets.

"That would be sad." He turned and glanced out her door to the lobby, his gaze resting on the floor-to-ceiling river stone fireplace. "I helped literally build this," he said to her over his shoulder. Then he shook his head and turned back around. "Every time I come here I remember me and Owen working side by side, and him talking about his dreams for the future. He was so excited."

Caroline rapidly blinked to keep her eyes from tearing up.

"The offer I made still stands. I think I could get some friends together and buy it from you. Keep your brother's dream alive without you having to turn your whole life upside down."

"Thank you. But this is where I need to be right now. For Owen's sake—and Dylan's."

Vincent cleared his throat. "I'll have time to help you run things. Since it looks like I'm going to be a single man again, I have some time on my hands."

He'd told her when he'd arrived at the office that his wife, Tiffany, had filed for divorce. Hearing the sorrow in his voice had made her realize how self-centered she'd become. Other people's troubles might not appear as dramatic as hers right now, but to them they were every bit as real and heartbreaking.

"Have you tried counseling?" she asked. "Owen's church has some very good programs." Not that she'd been able to attend church lately.

He shook his head, his expression grim. "It's going to take a lot more than talk to fix things between Tiffany and me." He walked out of her office and into the lobby where Dottie was putting some newly arrived advertising flyers into the holders on a display board.

"Caroline, it looks like your nine o'clock appointment is here," Zane called out. He'd been standing by the front door, keeping an eye on everything happening outside. Now he strode into her office. "Let me see the guy's picture on your computer screen to make sure it's him."

She pulled up the photo she had of the sports equipment supplier who was willing to cut her a deal if she placed her order today.

"Please don't frisk him when he comes in," she said while Zane leaned over her shoulder to study the picture.

He gave a little noncommittal grunt in response. He moved back into the lobby and she followed him.

Zane pushed open the door and headed down the front steps and toward the parking area. At the same time, the reserve officer who'd been stationed outside of the building got out of his patrol car. Zane and the officer walked over to the visiting salesman who'd just parked his truck with a small storage trailer attached to it.

Caroline cringed a little. She'd warned the salesman about the situation he was in. Fortunately, he was understanding. And eager to make a sale. Still, this paranoid greeting was not exactly the kind of first impression she'd wanted to make on a new business associate.

She watched the three men talking and soon the salesman was smiling and nodding his head. Soon after that, Zane escorted the salesman up the steps, helping him carry satchels that were presumably filled with samples of winter sports clothes, hats and gloves. The sports equipment samples she wanted to see must be in the trailer. The reserve officer remained outside, watching the long winding driveway that led from the service road along the lake and up to Wilderness Photo Adventures.

Three hours later, Caroline had placed her order and the salesman had left. Now the pressure was really on to get the business up and running in order to pay for all of the stuff she'd just bought.

She grabbed a small bottle of peach-flavored ice tea from the office fridge and walked back into the lobby while cracking the seal on the bottle and taking a couple of swigs.

"All right, Dottie, we're done," she called out. "I know it's been a stressful day and we've all been on eggshells wondering if some idiot was going to try and kill me again. I think we've put in enough work for now. Go on home and I'll pay you your full eight hours."

Her office manager looked up uncertainly from the pile of sales brochures she'd been folding.

"You better take me up on it," Caroline gently chided. "Pretty soon we'll be up and running with regular business hours and there'll be no cutting out early."

"Well, you make a good argument." Dottie started organizing the papers into neat piles. "Let me straighten this up a little and I'll go."

Caroline took another sip of tea. Zane's phone rang. He glanced at the screen and answered. Whatever the person on the other end said made Zane head toward the window. "I see it." To Caroline he said, "You didn't tell me you were expecting anybody else."

"I'm not."

Zane relayed that information into his phone and disconnected.

Caroline set down her bottle of tea. "What's wrong?"

"Jeff says there's a car coming up the drive and it's moving fast."

Caroline took a deep breath and tried to steady the panic that rose up in her stomach. "It might just be kids or tourists trying to drive around the lake. People sometimes don't realize they took the wrong fork at the junction and that they're now on a drive that dead-ends here on private property."

"It would have to be kids with a pretty good allowance," Zane said, looking out the window. "That's a very expensive car."

Caroline stepped up beside him but Zane gestured for her to move back. A few seconds later she saw a luxury sedan slide to a stop in the gravel.

The reserve officer had pulled his patrol car up near the building.

The sedan's door opened and a woman got out. She was tall and slender, with dark auburn hair. She wore a beautiful black suit that was exquisitely tailored.

"That's Rowena Sauceda," Caroline said. "The Chief Operations Officer for the Cobalt

Resort. She's called several times, offering to buy Wilderness Photo Adventures, and each time I've turned her down."

"Well, they say she doesn't take no for an answer." Dottie dropped the stack of papers she'd been holding onto her desk and sat down. "I'm hanging around for this."

"Stand back," Zane said to Caroline as Rowena Sauceda approached the door.

"Seriously?"

"Yes," Zane said grimly. "We can't afford to assume anything."

"True." It was foolish of her to think she could tell what a killer would look like. Anyone could be behind the attempts on her life. Even an executive at the resort.

Rowena walked through the door and quickly looked around until she saw Caroline. "You're a difficult lady to track down."

"That would be the point," Caroline said.

"Fair enough." Rowena glanced around at Zane, Dottie and Vincent. "Can we talk somewhere in private?"

"I'm afraid not." Caroline had been standing at the back of the lobby but now she stepped forward. The anxiety she'd felt just moments ago quickly turned to anger. Who was Rowena to barge in here when it was obvious Caroline wanted to be left alone? "How did you know I was here?"

"I paid a couple of my employees to keep an eye on the place and let me know if they saw any activity."

Fury burned the surface of Caroline's skin. What if those employees had been willing to share that information with someone else for extra money on the side—someone like her attacker? This self-centered woman could have gotten her killed. She bit her lip to keep from saying something she'd regret. "You found me. What do you want?"

"Your business. Name your price."

"It's not for sale."

"Oh, come on. Everything is for sale."

"That's not true." She put her hands on her hips. "Tell me exactly why you want this place so badly."

Rowena glanced out the window and Caroline got the impression she was carefully reviewing what she was about to say. And that maybe she was withholding something.

"There isn't a lot of lakeside property available at the moment. This place would be perfect for us. It can be seen from the docks behind our resort. Guests would be able to enjoy an array of outdoor activities. That's a huge draw these days, more so than we'd anticipated. You also have a nice sandy beach here. And since it used to be a campground, there are already good trails in place for hiking or snowshoeing.

"People on vacation want convenient, easy activities and we want to be able to offer them. Right now we don't have anything to provide other than boating, tennis courts and a small golf course." Rowena sighed. "So now that you know all of that, I'm sure it's obvious you can demand a high price and we'll pay it."

Caroline shook her head. "I haven't been trying to negotiate a higher price all this time. The property really isn't for sale."

Rowena stared at her for a moment and then frowned and shook her head. "If you change your mind, you let me know." She left as abruptly as she'd arrived.

"Well, isn't she a force of nature," Dottie muttered as soon as the door fell shut behind her.

Caroline wasn't sure what to think of Rowena Sauceda. Instead, she thought about the promise she'd made to Zane not to stay at the office for too long. If Rowena's employees were watching the business to report back to her, they could be reporting her position to someone else, too.

That thought made the hairs on the back

of Caroline's neck stand up. But she couldn't leave yet. There was a task she needed to take care of.

"Okay, guys, you can go," she said to Dottie and Vincent. "Thanks for your help."

"I'm not anxious to go back to an empty house," Vincent said. "I'll stay and help make sure you get into Zane's truck and get away safely."

"Oh, take a hint." Dottie walked up beside him and nudged him with her elbow. "They probably have something to do or talk about that isn't our business. Let's go. If you're lonesome you can go to the church play rehearsal with me and my kids. I thought they were going to have to miss it, so I'm glad to leave early." She grabbed his arm and pulled him outside before Caroline could hear his response.

Zane locked the door behind them and then turned to Caroline. "You ready to search the office and see if we can find anything?"

Caroline nodded. And later, when they were finished looking, she was both relieved and disappointed that they hadn't found anything.

"What about the outer buildings?" she asked him.

"I think we've been here long enough. We need to get you back up to the ranch."

He was right. "Okay, let's go."

The reserve officer following them in his patrol car stayed a discreet distance behind until they were north of town and it was clear they hadn't been followed. Then he turned back. She was grateful for all the time and effort people were putting in to keep her and her family safe—she just wished it wasn't necessary. When would all of this end?

On the ride back to the ranch, Caroline thought through all the things that had happened to her since she'd returned to Cobalt. She couldn't escape the feeling that the reasons for the attempts on her life were right in front of her. She just wasn't seeing them.

Zane wasn't thrilled to be back at the Bull Pine Tavern but if that's where his dad wanted to meet, so be it. He'd gotten a call from the bartender telling him he had two hours to get down to the tavern if he wanted to talk to Lee Coleman.

His dad had picked a Saturday night when the tavern was crowded and busy. Zane didn't know what to expect. He wasn't even sure how his dad would look. It had been a long time since they'd last seen each other and he'd both looked forward to and dreaded this moment for a while. If Caroline's life hadn't been in danger, he would probably have put off meeting him for at least another year. Maybe longer.

He glanced around in the dim light, broken up by neon beer signs and whatever images were flickering across the TV monitors placed around the bar, but he didn't see anyone who looked like his dad.

So he walked to the end of the bar and looked around the corner, to the area where the pool tables and electronic games were. It took him a minute, but he finally picked out a familiar slim figure leaning against a pool table. Something about the man's slouched posture and the tilt of his head caught Zane's attention.

Apparently the man saw Zane watching him at the same time. He stood and turned toward him, but didn't take a step forward. So that was the kind of reunion it was going to be. Hesitant and suspicious. Why should he expect anything different?

Zane moved closer. The people shooting pool continued shrieking and laughing, paying no attention at all to Zane as he walked between him. They didn't seem to be paying much attention to his dad, either, even though he was involved in their game. But then that's the kind of friends Lee Coleman generally had.

There was a small light fixture hanging low over the pool table, and Zane finally got close enough to see the crooked nose that had been broken numerous times and the lips twisted in a familiar, permanent scowl. "Hi, Pop."

Lee didn't make a move toward his son. "You wearing a wire? Working for the cops?"

"No."

It was hard to believe this was the man who had put so much fear into Zane at one time. Now he just looked small. And used up.

"Well, if you're lying and you really are working for the cops I just want to say I'm not involved in anything illegal and I don't know anybody who is."

Maybe that was true. Probably it wasn't.

"How are you?" Zane asked.

Lee shook his head. "You don't care."

Zane realized he actually did. Not only were the old fear and intimidation long gone, but to his surprise some of the old anger was gone, too—leaving room for compassion he hadn't expected to feel. He'd prayed for his dad on and off over the years. Starting now he would be more consistent about that. His father was obviously a tormented, burnt-out shell of a man.

"Can we talk privately?"

Lee grabbed his beer bottle from the edge of the pool table and led the way to a table in a corner. "If you're here for money, I don't have any," he said over his shoulder.

"I'm doing all right," Zane said after they sat down. Zane was flooded with gratitude for both the Heavenly Father who loved him and the surrogate earthly father, Sergeant Henry Marsh, who had helped him avoid living the life that Lee had.

"I hope you can help me with something," Zane said.

Lee's eyebrows raised slightly. It occurred to Zane that he might be asking for help from someone who was actually involved in the attacks. With his background, Lee could easily be a hired thug. One of the unseen shooters at the house. That would be like him. If the money was good enough, he'd do just about anything. And in this case, maybe he'd even take less pay just for a chance to hurt the Marshes. He might still carry a grudge against the family. Zane didn't want to believe that was the case, but it was possible. If there was any chance this could lead to information that would make Caroline safer, then asking for Lee's help was a chance he had to take.

"Do you know anything about the attempted hits on Caroline Marsh?"

Lee lifted one corner of his mouth in a half grin. "You still got a thing for that girl?"

"No." Zane wasn't still pining over the girl he walked out on years ago. That relationship was in the past—and the feelings he had for her now were new. More mature than the youthful infatuation he'd felt before. And they were surprisingly strong. The Caroline Marsh he knew now was impressive. She was tough. And beautiful. He quickly shoved that train of thought out of his mind.

"The police have traced one of the men who attacked her at the marina office complex back to a group out of Seattle," Zane said. "The other might still be in town. Have you heard anything about either of them? Or anything at all about any of the attacks on her or the murder of her brother?"

"No."

"Maybe the attackers were from around here, hired by outside people?"

Lee shook his head. "I don't want to go back to prison, so I don't spend any time around anybody like that anymore." He dragged a thumbnail over the label on his beer bottle. "I can ask around. I wasn't much of a father to you after your mom died." He cleared his throat. "I owe you."

Zane felt a little lurch in his stomach. That acknowledgment, coming from Lee Coleman, was big.

"Be careful," Zane said. "You warned me what happens to people who get too nosy."

Lee nodded. Then he took an old flip phone out of his pocket and asked for Zane's number. Zane gave it to him and told himself not to expect to hear anything back from Lee, not to get his hopes up. "If I hear anything, I'll let you know," Lee promised.

"Or just call me to talk," Zane said.

His dad laughed and shook his head.

Small steps. He asked his dad for his phone number. Lee gave him one. Maybe it was real. Maybe it was a fake. All he could do was accept it, and see what happened.

One of Lee's friends yelled to him from the pool table. Apparently it was his turn to shoot. Zane decided not to wear out his welcome. "Thanks for meeting with me."

Lee nodded then ambled over to his friends.

Zane left. When he got back to the ranch, Rose had a plate of baked ham and scalloped potatoes waiting for him. He ate it at the kitchen table, while Millie snored on the throw rug by the door. Playing with the other dogs at the ranch had worn her out.

Nobody asked him about his meeting with Lee, though they all knew where he'd been.

Eventually, he wandered into the den where Caroline sat on the sofa with an electronic tablet on her lap and the TV turned to an old movie.

"How was your dad?" she asked after a few minutes.

"He looks twice his age. Seems tired."

"Hard living will do that."

"Yeah. Reminds me of how blessed I am." And it reminded him of how determined he was to protect Caroline and her family. He wanted to go out of his way to help others, like Sergeant Henry. And he wanted to do the right thing for Caroline and for himself. All along, he'd been telling himself that that meant when this was over, he had to let her go. But was that true? They couldn't recapture what they'd had in the past, but was there a chance they could build something new? He wasn't sure. And now wasn't the time to figure it out. Not when he needed to keep all his focus on the danger at hand.

But in this moment, he could let himself enjoy just sitting beside her.

THIRTEEN

"I'm sorry, Caroline. I know it's not what you wanted to hear. But at this point I could see a judge giving Michelle at least some access to Dylan. And a shared custody arrangement is a possible outcome."

"But that's so *wrong*." Caroline couldn't help leaning across the table toward her lawyer. Hannah Romani looked so professional and composed that Caroline wasn't sure she grasped the realities of what she was suggesting and just how tragic it could be for a little boy who deserved so much more.

Their conversation had started twenty minutes ago, and so far Caroline hadn't heard much that made her happy.

"My former sister-in-law doesn't have a genuine interest in her son," Caroline added, hearing the pleading tone in her own voice. "She just wants the money. And the sad joke is on her. Right now there *isn't* any money. And

I'm not even certain Wilderness Photo Adventures will be up and running on the timetable I'd planned, so there might not be any money for a while yet."

She slid a sideways glance at Zane who was seated in a chair beside her. "All the more reason I *have* to get back to the office." She tried to keep the snippy tone out of her voice but failed. And the look of grave concern in his eyes made her ashamed of herself. It wasn't his fault she'd been holed up at the Rocking Star Ranch for the last week while trying to give Dottie directions over the phone and running into one problem after another.

She exhaled loudly in frustration. "I'm sorry, Zane," Caroline said quietly.

He nodded his acceptance of her apology. "I wish I could fix everything for you. And your family."

Michelle had filed the paperwork to gain custody of Dylan, and Caroline had immediately contacted Hannah to arrange an appointment—in person. There were some things you wanted to talk to an attorney about face-to-face. They were that important. She hadn't wanted to go back to Hannah's office at the lakeside office complex where she was first attacked and shot in the shoulder. The thought of being at the scene where it had all happened had made her too anxious. And she hadn't wanted to confirm to anyone that she was staying at the Rocking Star Ranch, even if most people in town who knew her and Zane could probably guess that was the case. So she'd had to find another place to meet with Hannah.

In the end, Hannah had arranged to talk with her here, in a coffee shop, at a table backed up into a corner. Hannah had been considerate enough to let Caroline and Zane sit facing the front door so they could see everyone who walked in.

"The family court judge likely won't dismiss Michelle's petition out of hand, though I'll start out by asking for that," Hannah continued. "My research shows your former sister-in-law has had several run-ins with the law but nothing that led to significant charges. Nothing that would automatically disqualify her from being able to take custody."

"What about her boyfriend? Everyone knows he's a criminal." Caroline wanted to scream the words, but she didn't. "And everyone knows Michelle uses drugs. Can't we demand a drug test?" She shoved herself back into her chair and crossed her arms. "A couple of months after Dylan was born she started wanting to spend more time with her friends, which seemed perfectly fine to Owen. But none of her close friends had children. They were free to do whatever they wanted, whenever they wanted. Eventually, Michelle decided that she'd made some wrong life decisions. That she didn't want to be a mother anymore. That woman wanted *nothing* to do with her son from the time he was eight months old until Owen died and she started thinking there might be some money up for grabs."

Her eyes began to water and she felt her chin quiver. She couldn't help it. "If Dylan spends any time with his mother he'll be in *danger*."

Hannah nodded her understanding. "No one wants that," she said firmly. "But I wanted you to be aware of all the possible outcomes. Not just the ones you're hoping for." She turned off her electronic tablet and tucked it into her satchel. "My office will do everything we can."

But that might not be enough. Caroline leaned forward, dropping her elbows onto the small round wooden table. "What if I just pay Michelle off? I don't have a lump of money I could give her right now, but maybe we could draw up some kind of contract. Once Wilderness Photo Adventures is up and going I could agree to pay her a percentage of the profit each month in return for her promising to stay away from Dylan."

Hannah sighed. "I cannot in good conscience advise you to do something like that."

"But it would probably resolve the issue, as far as making Michelle happy is concerned."

Hannah stood and plucked her leather satchel from the seat of the chair where she'd set it. "I hate to think that's true."

"But it probably is."

"Do not make Michelle a monetary offer yet," Hannah said. "Just sit tight and wait to hear from me." Then she left.

Caroline reached into her purse and pulled out her phone. "I might as well call Michelle and see how much money it's going to take."

Zane reached out and lightly rested his hand on her arm. "It sounds like Hannah wants you to leave it alone. Let her figure out the legal maneuverings for now."

"I don't think talking through lawyers is the way to go with Michelle. She might play games with the court system, but if I talk to her directly I think she'll give me a specific number that would make her willing to just go away. I won't promise her anything—I just want to know what range we're looking at. I can't sleep for worrying about this. I have so many other things to think about but my thoughts keep coming back to Dylan. Money could turn out to be an easy fix for the situation."

"You're probably right. She probably doesn't really want Dylan. Maybe she's choosing right now to stir things up for a reason. I'm not saying she's necessarily personally involved in the attacks, but who knows? Maybe someone's paying her to call you out. Get you to show up at a time and place she knows about in advance."

"But I can't let this continue through the court system. What if she wins custody?"

"I'm not telling you not to fight for Dylan. I'm just suggesting you be cautious until things settle down. Until we know you're safe." He removed his hand from her arm.

"All right." She sighed. "I've got to go back into the office this week." Caroline held her hand up when it looked like he was going to argue. "Bobby Boom wants to send a representative over to check everything out and make sure we're still on target to open in three weeks. I want to be there when he makes his visit."

Zane shook his head. "I don't like it."

"I don't either. But there are some things I need to take care of that no one else can do. Things that can't be accomplished online. At least this time a visit won't set off any alarms for Rowena Sauceda's spies or anyone else who might be watching. There's activity going on there all the time now with Dottie showing up every weekday and some of the staff we've hired coming in for training and paperwork. We can pick a random time to meet with the guy. Make it quick."

When he frowned at her she squared her shoulders. "It's for Dylan. And Mom, too." It was strange to think how the roles had switched around and now it was up to her to take care of her family.

Finally, Zane nodded. "Well, first things first. Dylan and your mom are expecting us at Rennie's for a quick visit. He'll be disappointed that Millie isn't with us, but I recorded her playing with the ranch dogs and that crazy gray barn cat on my camera." He smiled a little bit. "I can't wait to show him."

Really? He'd thought of that? Despite the anxiety gripping her whole body, she felt her heart melt. It was obvious Dylan was fascinated with Zane. And good to know the feeling of friendship was reciprocated.

Zane took out his phone and started tapping a text message. "I'll let Matt know we're getting ready to go."

As a precaution, they'd borrowed a car from

Zane's friend, Patrick. Zane had let Matt know the day before that they were driving into town and Matt had arranged to have himself assigned to patrol near the coffee shop and then near Rennie's home. Just in case.

A minute later Zane's phone pinged and he looked up. "Matt's ready. Let's go see your mom and Dylan."

Four days later, Caroline was still thinking about the custody situation with Dylan and Michelle when she glanced up and saw Vincent rubbing his hands over his arms. "It is definitely turning colder. And you can see the days are getting shorter." He turned from the window at the front of Wilderness Photo Adventures and gestured behind him at the lake. "But it doesn't matter what the season is. That, out there, is always beautiful."

Caroline glanced back at the stack of paper invoices she was scanning and nodded. "Hopefully, we can get a little more consistent in posting daily pictures online of the beautiful view. It might help entice people to pay us a visit." She glanced over at Dottie who was on the other side of the office. She had her phone pressed to her ear, apparently trying to break up an argument between a couple of her kids who were fighting over whose turn it was to wash the dishes.

Dottie was understandably overwhelmed by all the responsibilities that were being placed on her shoulders while Caroline couldn't come to the office. Posting a few new pictures to their website every day to show the changing seasons was one of Dottie's tasks that had fallen by the wayside. All things considered, Caroline figured she could just let it slide for now.

In the four days since meeting with her attorney at the coffee shop, Caroline had done all the online preparation for the official company opening that she possibly could. She'd do whatever it took to make sure Wilderness Photo Adventures made enough money that she could pay off Michelle if she had to.

"Well, we're getting to the time of year when my construction work dies down in this part of the country. And with everything going on between me and Tiffany, there's no way I'm taking jobs very far away." Vincent looked down at his feet. "I'm happy to come out here and help as much as I can. Maybe it will keep my mind off things."

Caroline set the invoices down on her desk and gave him her full attention. Once again, she'd let herself get so caught up in her own troubles that she'd practically forgotten other people had problems, too. "You and Tiffany haven't worked things out?"

He shook his head sadly and looked up at her. "Not yet."

"Keep praying."

He crossed his arms. "Praying is fine, but I'm looking at practical things, too. Changes to our lifestyle that I'm sure will make her a lot happier." He nodded a couple of times, as if reaffirming his commitment to fixing his marriage. Then he reached into his back pocket, pulled out a box knife and walked over to a stack of boxes. He cut the seal on one and started pulling out plastic-wrapped sweatshirts with the Wilderness Photo Adventures logo stamped on the front.

As an extra source of income, Wilderness Photo Adventures would be selling clothes, hats, gloves, survival gear and camera equipment, among other things. Dottie had no retail experience and one of the reasons Caroline needed to come by today was to give her a quick tutorial on merchandising.

While she watched Vincent work at setting up the displays, Caroline said a quick prayer for him and Tiffany.

Dottie finished her phone conversation and then brought Caroline a mug of coffee and set it on her desk. "No offense, but when are you going to get out of here? Bobby Boom's assistant, or whatever he is, left an hour ago."

Caroline glanced at her over the rim of her mug while she took a sip. Bobby Boom's representative had been visibly stunned at Dottie's lack of finesse regarding social media. Dottie hadn't taken to that too well and had pressed her lips together until they turned white. Beyond that, the visit had gone well. Seeing Caroline in the office and confirming that they truly were moving forward with the business and would be opening on time seemed to satisfy him.

"You're never going to get it perfect," Dottie said, pulling a chair over and sitting next to her. "And despite what that *kid* associate Bobby Boom sent over seemed to think, I'm not a complete idiot. If you explain things to me, I can do them." Her words were grumbly but she wore a genuine smile on her face.

"I know. I just need to take care of a couple more things."

Caroline and Zane had arrived with their police escort an hour ahead of Dottie and Vincent. Zane's assignment on this trip was to search the outer buildings, which included storage sheds, several tent cabins and a cafeteria for anything Owen might have hidden there. The tent cabins and cafeteria buildings were closed off until Caroline could afford to get them upgraded and made usable sometime in the future.

As far as Dottie and Vincent knew, Zane was out there taking pictures so Caroline could send them off to get remodeling estimates.

Curiosity over what Zane might be finding as he dug deep into those buildings ate at Caroline. Much as she'd wanted to look through them herself, she'd had to agree with him that for her to walk around on the property was taking an unreasonable risk. The police department had agreed to send a reserve officer to protect her only if she took the precaution of staying inside the office. The cop had been ordered to stage his patrol car at the point where the long private driveway met the lakeside road, about a half-mile away.

In return for Caroline's promise to stay inside and keep the office doors locked, Zane had agreed to record his search of the buildings and send her short bursts of video. She'd already looked at a couple of small snippets, both hopeful and fearful she'd see something suspicious or important. So far, she hadn't. Early on, maybe she hadn't really wanted to know the truth about her brother and what had gotten him killed. Not if it had painted an ugly picture of the Owen she'd loved. But now she was willing to face anything if that was what it took for the nightmare to end.

Fear lingered in the back of her mind all the time, now. Like some kind of low-volume electrical buzzing sound that made it hard to concentrate and left her feeling edgy and restless.

She was already weary of living like this, having to be cautious with her every move and being forced to live in seclusion. What if the attacks couldn't be stopped? What if she had to live like this for the rest of her life?

Dottie reached over and set a napkin on Caroline's keyboard. Then she dropped a couple of the bakery cookies she kept hidden in her desk on top of it. Caroline sat back and tried to smile. "Thanks, Dottie, but I can't eat anything right now."

"Well, at least I got half my mission accomplished. You stopped working and worrying for a minute."

"I'm all right."

"There's only so much you can control with this business," Dottie said. "You can do everything you intend to do, but what if we get one of those freakish winters where we don't get much snow? Maybe get a bunch of rain instead. No one's going to pay to come up here and tromp around in mountain mud."

"Wow, thanks for cheering me up." Caroline wrapped up her cookies in the napkin and set it aside.

Dottie smiled and titled her head slightly. "Honey, I'm just saying you do what you can do. If trouble comes, if we have a bad winter or mess up the *social media* or whatever, we'll just pick ourselves up and try again. And ahead of all of that, we're going to have faith."

Caroline nodded and felt her eyes tear up. She was grateful for this new friendship with Dottie and grateful that Owen had found someone like her to help with his dream.

But Dottie didn't know about Michelle's threat to take Dylan. Her attempt at gaining custody. Caroline *had* to get the money to pay her off. Wilderness Photo Adventures *had* to be a success.

Her phone chimed. It was Zane letting her know he'd finished recording his last video. He was approaching the door and would need her to unlock it to let him in.

"What do you think?" she asked him in a quiet voice as he walked up to her at the front door. "Did you find anything unusual?"

"You'll have to look at the video and tell me what you think," he answered, using the same quiet tone so the others wouldn't hear. "But I didn't see anything that looked suspicious. I opened every door I could and checked for loose floorboards where somebody might've hidden something, but it was a wash."

"What about looking in the actual ground on the property? Maybe something is buried in the dirt. Or under a rock or—"

Zane reached for both her hands and took them in his. "I'm sorry, but that kind of search just isn't practical. This property is over a hundred acres, most of it covered with thick forest."

Caroline bit the side of her cheek to keep from bursting into tears. She didn't realize until now how much she'd gotten her hopes up that they'd find something. That it would all be over.

"We don't even have a solid reason to believe there's anything hidden here at all. Or hidden anywhere else." He squeezed her hands. "It's a theory we had. That's all."

Caroline nodded, trying not to let the crashing sense of disappointment drag her down.

Vincent walked over to them with his phone in his hand. "Are we about ready to wrap things up here? It looks like I might have plans for dinner."

Caroline turned to him. "Sure." Then she

called over to Dottie to let her know it was time to go.

Behind her, she heard Zane on his phone calling the officer at the end of the long driveway to let him know they would be leaving.

Once everyone was outside, Caroline set the alarm and locked the front door. The temperature had dropped and dark clouds on the northwest horizon appeared to be moving toward Cobalt. Dottie and Vincent both waved their good-byes and started to walk toward their vehicles.

Caroline glanced over at the last slivers of late afternoon sunlight shining on the surface of the lake as she walked beside Zane toward his pickup truck. There were still a few diehard boaters out there, enjoying the last days before it got too cold to take a boat out. The crisp air felt cool on her face. It made her feel a little more energetic. Even a little excited about the upcoming holidays.

Next fall, maybe Wilderness Photo Adventures could offer an easy walking tour with opportunities to photograph fall foliage and then maybe a bonfire with s'mores at the very end. That might be fun.

She heard a loud *crack* and something ripped a small branch off the pine tree right beside her head.

FOURTEEN

"Gun!" Zane grabbed Caroline around the waist and pulled her to the ground, shielding her body with his. Where were the shots coming from? He raised his head to look around, only to hear another shot and see it ricochet off the ground within inches of Caroline's head.

The lake. That had to be the direction the assassin was firing from. He hoped Vincent and Dottie had both taken cover somewhere but he couldn't look for them right now. He quickly glanced around for some kind of barrier that would protect Caroline from the shooter. His truck was too far away and the few pine trees near them were too sparse and skinny.

The storage shed at the end of dock was his best option. Keeping his arm wrapped around Caroline, he pointed to where they were going and then pulled her up and alongside him as he ran. He pulled at the storage shed's door but it wouldn't budge. He remembered he'd locked the door after he finished checking its contents earlier in the day. Then he'd given the keys back to Caroline and he'd seen her drop them into her desk drawer. At least he had his gun and he pulled it out from beneath his jacket while he crouched down beside Caroline, staying as low as possible.

"Are you hurt?" he asked Caroline.

Her eyes were huge and her face was pale, but she shook her head. "No. I'm all right."

The sound of Dottie shrieking reached his ears just before she rounded the corner of the small building and slid to the ground beside them. She was out of breath, and a few seconds passed before she was able to reassure Zane that she was all right.

By the time she responded he was already on his phone, talking to the cop at the end of the drive and describing what he'd just witnessed. The patrol car raced up the drive.

For some reason Lee's comment about Zane still having a thing for Caroline ran through Zane's mind. Lee had threatened Caroline and her family before because of Zane's closeness to them. And now that he was close to them again… Maybe it was his dad who took those shots. They came from the lake. It was difficult to target someone on land from an unsteady boat, but the shooter had come remarkably close. If his dad was sober he could have made that shot. At least he could have in the old days, when he was a skilled cowboy.

"Did you see that?" Vincent shouted, running across the parking lot toward the cop car and pointing toward the lake.

Zane cautiously came out from behind the shed and looked in the direction Vincent was pointing. There were several boats on the water, but none was particularly close.

"There!" Vincent pointed toward a powerboat some distance away, leaving a churning white wake as it headed toward the resort docks.

Zane could hear the cop on his radio, calling in an update on the situation and advising that a potential suspect was heading toward the resort.

"Rowena Sauceda!" Vincent shouted as he came to a stop near the officer. "The shooter was Rowena Sauceda!"

Zane headed toward them. Caroline and Dottie slowly came out from behind the shed and also walked toward the officer.

"You're talking about the executive from the resort?" the cop asked.

Vincent nodded.

"How could you tell?" Zane asked.

"That hair. Bright red. Looked like she had a scarf tied over it but it blew back when she sped away. Tall, slender. I'm telling you, I saw her taking that second shot."

Caroline stood beside Zane and reached for his hand. "Could it really be her behind all of this?" she asked, sounding stunned by the thought.

"The Cobalt resort enticed her away from the fancy place in Hawaii where she was working by offering her a stake in ownership here," Vincent said. "Everybody knows that. It was a big deal when she came to town."

Caroline squeezed Zane's hand.

"Let's go!" Vincent said. "Let's meet the cops at the resort before she can slip away. I can identify her."

The cop was on his radio identifying Rowena Sauceda as his potential suspect and asking she be held for questioning.

"If it really is her, I want to see her arrested," Caroline said, turning to Zane.

"You need to let the police take care of this," the officer said. He looked at Vincent until he had his complete attention.

"I'm not going to get in the way," Vincent said, lowering the volume of his voice and calming down a little. "I just want to make it clear that I *saw* her do it. She's a danger to Caroline and a danger to this town. And if you need to ask me questions for your report, you can ask me over at the resort. Because that's where I'm going."

Vincent strode over to his truck.

"I'm going, too," Caroline said. She turned to give Zane a challenging look. "Do I need to ask Vincent for a ride?"

Zane held onto her hand. "If you're determined to go, I'll drive you."

"You coming?" Caroline asked Dottie.

Her office manager shook her head. "I just want to go home. Call me if you need me."

Zane and Caroline got into his truck and he started up the engine. At least his dad wasn't the shooter. It was a relief to know that.

"Rowena certainly has the money to hire the thugs who have been after me," Caroline mused aloud.

Zane heard her sigh and he reached his arm over and wrapped it around her shoulder.

"All of this heartbreak just because of greed," she said sadly.

The front of the resort was filled with vehicles, including several patrol cars, so Zane parked in the lot not far from Vincent's truck.

They walked into the lobby. The back wall was floor-to-ceiling glass with a beautiful view of the lake, the resort's docks and an outdoor patio restaurant.

An elevator chimed and the doors slid open. Rowena stepped out with officers flanking her.

"She's the shooter!" Vincent yelled, elbowing his way past employees and resort guests who stopped to gawk. "I saw her!"

Rowena looked stunned. She stared straight ahead as the officers escorted her outside to a patrol car. Several people took pictures of the event with their phones.

A detective Zane had worked with a couple of times walked up to him. "I need to talk to you."

"Sure."

The detective glanced at Caroline. "Alone." He gestured in the direction of a small conference room. "I'll make it quick."

"She comes with me," Zane said.

The detective shook his head. "You know standard procedure is to talk to witnesses separately. I want to talk to you first. Then I'll talk to Ms. Marsh. We want a tight investigation from start to finish—no shortcuts or loose threads a lawyer could use to question things later."

"Go with him," Caroline said. "He's right. We want a solid investigation and I really want this to be over." She gestured toward the lobby. "There are cops everywhere. I'll be fine."

Zane nodded, suddenly struck by the realization that he didn't really want to go anywhere without her. Ever. His heart seemed to swell a little in his chest as he took a last lingering look at her. Then he followed the detective into the conference room.

Caroline sat on a sofa in the lobby of the resort and hugged her arms tightly against her chest. In the race to get over here and make sure the police arrested Rowena, she'd been fully focused on capturing the person responsible for all of the horrible things that had happened to her and her family, starting with Owen's murder.

Now she was thinking about how close she'd come to being shot. Again. *Thank You, Lord, for protecting me and everyone who was with me today.* The spot on the tree where the branch had been shot off hadn't been far from her head. Now that the shock had worn off, the realization of what could have happened had her trembling.

"Caroline!" Vincent called out through the crowd of people now filling the lobby. He strode over to her.

The last time she'd seen him he'd been walking down to one of the resort's first-floor business offices, talking to a cop. He must have finished giving his statement already. That was quick, but then he couldn't have had much to say. Caroline wouldn't have much to say, either, when it was her turn.

Caroline stood. "How's it—"

"Why aren't you answering your phone?" He cut her off before she could finish.

"Oh. I didn't even hear it ring." She started to reach into her purse for her phone but he took hold of her hand. Surprised, she looked up at him.

"Your mom called me and said she's been trying to contact you." His brows were lowered and his expression was worried. "Dylan has had a bad asthma attack."

"What?" A quick jolt of panic made it hard to think clearly. Had she known her nephew had asthma and forgotten about it? Owen had been diagnosed with asthma when he was in middle school, but his had been a relatively mild condition and he'd always been able to keep it under control. Was that the case with Dylan? Or was his condition more serious? Why couldn't she remember?

Caroline's life had become a whirlwind of terrifying events. Sometimes it felt like her mind had been spinning from the moment she got that call notifying her of Owen's death. She must have forgotten about Dylan's asthma. She shook her head. She was a bad aunt. So much for thinking Dylan would be safe in her care.

"He's at the hospital," Vincent continued, still holding her hand and giving it a reassuring squeeze. "I'm sure the doctors will take good care of him. But if you want to go to him, I can drive you."

"Okay," she said. What must the poor boy be going through? And what about her mom? How much stress could her heart take?

Vincent let go of her hand and took a couple of steps back. "Is Zane still giving his statement? We can wait for him if you'd rather do that."

"I want you to drive me to the hospital," she said, raising her voice so he could hear her over the din of noise in the lobby. Two resort hotel employees were standing nearby and one glanced over at her.

"All right," Vincent said, also raising his voice to be heard. "My truck is in the parking lot." He gestured for her to lead the way and then followed along behind her as she hurried across the lobby and out the door.

"I'm parked this way." He was moving

fast—she had to jog to keep up with him. Storm clouds had settled over town and icy rain was falling. Fear rose up in her throat, feeling like it could almost choke her. What must Vincent not be telling her about Dylan that had him in such a hurry?

"Are you sure it's an asthma attack?" she called out from behind him. Maybe it was something worse. Maybe there had been an attack on Dylan and her mom. Obviously Rowena wasn't in this alone. She must have hired people to help her. And those hired thugs could be anywhere.

They got to his truck. She slid into the passenger seat while he fired up the engine and started to back out.

She fastened her seatbelt, then reached into her purse for her phone. The battery was probably dead. She must have forgotten to charge it. That was the only reason she could think of that her mom wouldn't be able to get a call through.

But the screen lit up at her touch and it didn't show any missed calls. That was odd. Why would her mother call Vincent but not call her?

The old truck rocked on worn suspension as they crossed the parking lot and Caroline had to set her phone in her lap and hang on to keep from getting knocked around. It bounced again, harder, as they crossed out of the parking lot and onto the street. Once they were on the road, Vincent eased his foot off the accelerator, reached over and grabbed the phone from Caroline's lap. He tossed it to the floorboard and then kicked it under his seat.

"What?" Caroline turned to him and felt her jaw drop as she tried to comprehend what was happening. "Why did you do that?"

"You don't need to talk to anybody." Vincent raked a hand through his hair, then made a turn that took them away from the hospital in the center of town and toward the lake instead.

Oh, no. Confused, but determined to get out of the truck, Caroline reached for her door handle. Before she could pull it she felt something jam into her side near her waist. She knew it was a gun barrel even before she looked down at it.

"You try to jump out and I'll kill you right now," Vincent said. "I've got no reason not to."

The storm had turned the sky black. No one glancing into the truck would be able to see that she was in trouble. "Vincent, what are you doing?"

"Getting my life put back together."

"What are you talking about?" There were

other cars on the road, their headlights a passing blur in the rain. Maybe it would be worth taking the chance to jump out before he picked up speed. Maybe he wouldn't really shoot her.

She glanced over at him. In the dim light from the instrument panel she could see that his brows were furrowed and his chin dipped down. He was hunched over the steering wheel, looking like a cornered animal preparing to attack. This person was nothing like the helpful, humble man who'd met her and her mom and Dylan at the airport and driven them to town after Owen died. This was someone completely and frighteningly different.

What did she know about hostage situations? Kidnappings? As the daughter of a cop, she'd heard her dad tell her mom about the training he'd gone through at work and when it seemed especially interesting Caroline had listened in.

Think!

She should keep talking. Personalize herself. Make Vincent continue to see her as a fellow human being. Maybe that would keep him from going too far.

"Is Dylan really in the hospital?" she asked.

Vincent leaned back a little from the steering wheel and sighed. But he didn't look at her and that was worrisome. If he was trying to stay emotionally detached from her that was a very bad sign.

"Your mom and Dylan are fine," he said in a flat tone. "As far as I know."

What did that mean? "Is there someone else involved in this, in whatever's happening?"

He nodded. "Mrs. Marsh and Dylan will be fine," he said quietly, like he was talking to himself rather than to Caroline. "She'll sell the property after you're gone. We'll make sure she gets a good price."

"We? *Who?*"

He didn't answer and her thoughts raced with possibilities. "Rowena? Do you mean the resort will buy it?" But he'd just helped to get Rowena arrested. Why would he do that if they were working together? None of this was making any sense.

"Maybe." He grinned slightly. "That was pretty good, huh? Making it look like Rowena shot you from the boat? I got the idea after she barged into the office the last time you were there. It would be easy enough to say that I saw her. And just in case anyone else was looking at the right moment, the real shooter wore a red wig."

"Bobby Boom?" she asked. "Does he want to buy Wilderness Photo Adventures and own it himself?" Maybe he was behind all of this.

Vincent scoffed. "He has a lot of money, but he doesn't have *that* kind of money. Forget the business. Do you realize the value of the land?"

"Yes. A lot of it is lakefront property. It's a prime spot."

"*The* prime spot. You've been down in California for the last few years and that's kept you out of touch. Cobalt, Idaho, has become a prime location. Property prices are going up. The population keeps growing."

"I know that," she said, to keep him talking. "But I still don't understand what you're doing or why."

"You know the property Wilderness Photo Adventures is built on used to be a private campground. A hundred and ten acres. A good stretch of it on sandy beach along the lake. The family who owned it sold it to Owen for next to nothing. Your dad had helped them several times over the years and they wanted to pay tribute to him by helping Owen."

She imagined her dad. His time had been cut short, but he'd done a lot of good in the years he'd had.

"Not too long ago, the city changed a bunch of zoning laws, trying to keep the town from getting overbuilt. After that, the value of lakefront property skyrocketed. I tried to get your brother to sell the property, but you know what he told me? He said if he ever sold it, he'd sell it back to a member of the family that had originally sold it to him. And he'd only ask for the same low price that he'd paid for it."

That sounded like Owen.

Slowly, she was starting to piece things together.

"So you figured if Owen and his scruples were out of the way, then with your ten percent ownership you'd make ten percent of the profit when the property was sold? And you killed my brother for *that*?"

"You don't understand." His demeanor was changing. Now, instead of angry and brooding, he seemed agitated and anxious for her to understand him.

"So explain it to me."

"This isn't about greed. It's about me holding on to my family. Tiffany had been threatening to leave me for a long time before she finally moved out. She said she wasn't happy. But I *knew* I could make her happy if I just had more money. If your brother would have just sold the property at a reasonable price, my ten percent share would have saved my marriage and my life." His voice broke on the last word. "I can't live without her."

So it *was* about greed—a belief that money

would solve all the problems for a distraught man with disturbing priorities. Caroline didn't question him. Instead, she kept quiet so he would continue to talk while she came up with a plan to stay alive.

Vincent raked his fingers through his short hair several times. "A friend put me in contact with some people over on the coast. Business people who maybe cut some corners or get a little rough, but what do I care? They're interested in paying big money for that land and reselling it for huge money. So I tricked Owen into coming to Seattle for a meeting. When we got there, the business people laid out their offer to buy the property. Owen was furious and turned them down.

"Afterward, we were walking along the waterfront. It was raining, of course. It was Seattle. Owen told me he would never, ever sell the property for a profit. I got mad and shoved him. He fell and hit his head."

Caroline drew in a shaky breath. She didn't really want to hear the rest.

"Nobody was looking, so I rolled him over into the bay."

Lord, Caroline pleaded, *I pray for Your presence and protection. And I pray that Owen will know how much I love and miss him.*

"It turned out one of the guys from the

meeting had followed us," Vincent continued. "He saw everything, and said I had to do whatever he asked or he'd turn me into the cops for murder. I tried and tried to get you to sell, so it would all be over and everyone would be safe, but you wouldn't give in. They were the people who hired the two guys who were supposed to kill you outside your lawyer's office. After the one got caught and his partner killed him so he wouldn't talk to the cops, they made *me* work with that second guy."

So Vincent had been involved in the attack at her house.

"And you went along with all of this?"

He shrugged. "What else was I supposed to do? Go to jail? Lose everything? I *am* going to win my wife back. I'll buy her anything she wants. And don't worry, I'll look after your mom and Dylan, too. It's just your time to go. Like it was just Owen's time to go."

He had built up rationalizations for his behavior to the point of insanity. Caroline would not be able to save herself by reasoning with him. "The cops are probably already looking for you," she said. "And I'm sure Zane has noticed I'm gone by now."

"Maybe." He shrugged again. "But nobody will suspect me of doing anything to you. If they look at the lobby video, they'll see you walking ahead of me. Same thing with video outside the building. I made sure somebody in the lobby heard you asking me to take you to the hospital. And that will be my story. You demanded to be taken to the hospital for some reason—you didn't say why. I dropped you off outside the entrance and went to park. I never saw you again."

"You won't get away with it."

"With what? Killing you?" He shook his head. "I'm not going to kill you. I don't want any forensic evidence on me. I'm just going to lock you up for a little while. Someone else will take care of you. But don't worry. He's a pro. He'll make it quick."

They were on the south side of the lake now. There were homes out here in the forest, but none of them were close to the road. There wasn't much traffic this time of night. "Are we headed to Wilderness Photo Adventures?" Was that where he intended to lock her up?

He sat up straighter, his demeanor changing again. "I've said enough."

He still held his gun pointed at her, but he'd lowered it so that his hand was resting on the seat. Caroline figured she had nothing to lose by trying something. Anything. Her dad would tell her that. *Don't you ever quit.*

She took a deep breath, then shoved away his gun hand while at the same time she grabbed the steering wheel and sent the truck careening toward the forest. There was a loud blast as the gun fired through the windshield. Vincent pulled on the steering wheel while Caroline released her seatbelt, lunged for the door handle, yanked it open and leapt out.

FIFTEEN

"Why would Caroline ask Vincent to drive her to the hospital?" Matt muttered.

Zane stood beside the police sergeant in the security center for Cobalt Community Hospital. There were eight screens in front of them, each split into four different views. The hospital's chief of security ran the footage from the previous thirty minutes while they all looked for signs of Caroline. Meanwhile, officers and volunteers were combing the hospital and the surrounding grounds and buildings looking for her.

Fear and dread sat heavy and dense in the pit of Zane's stomach. He should never, ever have left her alone for a second. It was his fault she was in danger.

He cleared his throat. He'd just stepped into the room after talking to Mrs. Marsh on the phone. "Caroline's mother hasn't had any contact with her since about one o'clock this afternoon. And she has no idea why Caroline would want to go to the hospital." He crossed his arms over his chest and shifted his weight back and forth, anxious to get out of this little room and *do* something to find Caroline.

"Did you tell Mrs. Marsh we were sending a patrol car to station outside her friend's house to make sure she and the little boy were kept safe?"

"I did." Zane ground out the words, anger tightening his jaw muscles.

Cold fear had come at his chest like a sledgehammer when he'd walked out of his interview with the detective at the resort and didn't see Caroline waiting for him. He'd nearly bitten off the head of the first uniformed officer he'd found in the lobby, demanding to know who was keeping an eye on her. He'd been politely reminded that the officer he was glowering at had not been assigned to watch her. Nor had the officer been told Caroline was not to leave the building.

It was true. No one had been assigned to keep track of her. And it had not occurred to Zane to remind her not to leave without him.

"Somebody tricked her," Zane said, watching the security footage roll by in fast-forward. "She's a smart woman, but even a smart person can be fooled. Any of us can. Obviously." Self-disgust ripped through him. He'd been fooled, too. They all had.

Rowena Sauceda had an airtight alibi. She couldn't have taken that shot from the boat on the lake. She'd been in a meeting with four other people in the executive offices on the fifth floor.

The burning question now was, had Vincent been fooled, as well? Had someone tricked them into leaving the resort and then grabbed the both of them? Vincent was seen following Caroline out of the building. Lobby and outdoor security video at the resort confirmed that Caroline had been leading the way. Witnesses had heard her asking him to drive her to the hospital. So was he a victim as well, or was he part of some kind of setup?

A patrol car had been sent to Vincent's home and others were looking for his truck on the roads around town. The police department had called in the county sheriff's department for assistance. It had been only twenty minutes at most since Zane realized Caroline was missing and sent out the alarm. Fortunately the hospital was only a couple of blocks from the resort, but it had felt a lot farther when he was on his way over here hoping to find her safe and sound.

Matt thanked the hospital's chief of security

and asked him to keep an eye out for Caroline and Vincent. He provided digital pictures that had come from their driver's license records.

Zane and Matt were walking down one of the hospital's long corridors when Matt's phone chimed and he answered. "Got it," he said, and then disconnected.

"What?" Zane demanded. He had his own phone in his hand. He was getting ready to hit the button for Caroline, hoping she would finally pick up and dreading the moment if it rolled over to voice mail yet again.

"Dispatch pinged her cell phone," Matt answered. "Thanks to the rough terrain and the spotty cell coverage around here it took a couple of tries, but they located her phone on the south side of the lake."

They hurried down the hallway to the exit, jogged to Matt's patrol car once they were outside and took off with full lights and sirens. Icy rain was falling, making the road slick. The patrol car slid a little in the turns as they rounded the curves in the road.

Finally, they spotted flashing blue-and-red lights up ahead. Matt called dispatch to note their arrival and ask for another patrol car. A Jefferson County deputy sheriff in an SUV was parked at the side of the road. Vincent's truck was halfway off the asphalt a couple of feet away from it. The deputy had the flood-lights on the crossbar of her vehicle turned on high so she could see into the woods. She'd drawn her handgun.

They got out of the patrol car and Zane's attention focused on Vincent's truck. The windshield was blown out by what seemed to be a gunshot. Multiple scrapes and a deep gash in the front fender marked where it had apparently hit at least one of the nearby rock outcroppings along the side of the road. He walked over to take a closer look while Matt walked over to the deputy. Both of the truck's doors hung open. On the seat and dashboard he saw blood. For a moment he felt like his heart had stopped.

Lord, please let Caroline be all right.

The deputy had seen neither Caroline nor Vincent. Zane walked over to where she and Matt were standing, then he walked past them, looking for footprints in the mud leading into the woods. "What do you think?" Zane called out as he looked around the area that was lit up by the deputy's floodlights. "Were they driving and someone shot through the window?" It looked like they were together and someone was after them.

"This is odd," Matt said. "Looking at the

glass fragments, I'd stay somebody inside fired a shot *out* through the front windshield."

Zane felt fear harden in the pit of his stomach. "Could you get another ping on her phone?" he asked. "Maybe an update on where it is?"

A patrol car rolled up. Two officers got out. One of them walked over to Vincent's truck. He turned on a flashlight and looked around inside. Within a couple of minutes he shouted that he saw a cell phone on the floor. He called Zane over to have a look at it without picking it up. Zane's breath caught in his throat when he saw it. It was definitely Caroline's phone. The same officer looked around a little more and found Caroline's purse.

"They could have gotten into another vehicle," Matt said. "But they could also have headed into the woods." He got on the radio to call for a K-9 officer.

The dog and handler were already on a call, so it would take some time for them to arrive.

Zane was a tracker. And he wasn't about to stand around waiting. He told Matt he was going to start searching for her. Then he grabbed a flashlight from Matt's patrol car, walked to the edge of the area illuminated by the deputy's lights and began looking for footprints.

He whispered a quick prayer and scanned

the ground. The sleet that had been falling steadily for about an hour was starting to accumulate, threatening to cover any tracks. In an area where the ground was sheltered by some trees he finally found two sets of tracks that appeared to overlap and then diverge in different directions. He showed Matt what he'd found.

"You're the expect tracker," Matt said. "Which set of tracks do you want to follow? I'll try to follow whichever ones you don't choose."

The tracks weren't exactly clear. Rocks and pine straw made it hard to determine which were the smaller prints belonging to Caroline. The wrong choice would send him in the wrong direction. And that delay could get Caroline killed.

Caroline couldn't keep her teeth from chattering, which made it hard to hear if Vincent was gaining on her.

The night was bitterly cold and the icy rain had soaked her clothes. There was no way she could stay out all night and survive. Her hands and feet were already getting numb and she'd fumbled and fallen several times. She couldn't make it to the houses she knew were just over the ridge. The ground was too difficult to climb now that it was turning to mud and her feet kept sinking into it.

She made herself stop and hunker down behind a fallen blue spruce to regroup and think. *What do I do?*

She'd heard Vincent in the distance just a few minutes ago, and terror had set her heart pounding so hard she was afraid he would hear it. He'd called her name. Taunted her by offering to make her death a quick and painless one if she would just step out into the open.

He'd finally stopped talking, but she could still hear him. As he moved through the forest he snapped branches and occasionally sent rocks tumbling. Which meant if he ever decided to stop and listen while she was on the move, he'd likely hear *her*. Especially with her numb hands and feet making her so clumsy.

Why hadn't she called Zane to come with them when she thought Vincent was taking her to the hospital to see Dylan? How could she have been so foolish?

Another twig snapped. He was getting closer. She tried to breathe quietly even though nerves and exhaustion made her want to gasp for air. She didn't have time to give in to her fears. She needed a plan.

When she'd hit the ground after leaping out

of the truck, she'd rolled and scraped her hip and knee. But she'd been able to get up and run into the forest, away from the lake and toward the houses. At first rain dripping down into her eyes had made it hard to see. After wiping it away a couple of times and seeing the blood mixed with rain on her hands, she'd realized she must have gotten some cuts from the broken glass when Vincent shot out the windshield.

What if she backtracked toward the road and then headed toward the Wilderness Photo Adventures office? She could stay in the forest but walk parallel to the road where the ground was more level and she could move faster. Even if Vincent went back to his truck—assuming it was still drivable—and drove it up to the office, she would know when he went past her on the road. And she could turn and go in a different direction.

Was it a good plan? The cold air and her chilled, damp clothes clinging to her skin were draining her energy and making her thoughts foggy.

She heard the sound of a tree branch being moved and water droplets being shaken loose and falling to the ground. Vincent. Or maybe he'd called some of his cohorts to help track her down.

She was not going to sit here, trapped by indecision, until he found and killed her.

Slowly, she rose up and started to head back in the direction of the lakeside road. She reached a small rise covered with pine debris, stepped on it and sank down. Then she began to slide backward. A whimper escaped her.

No. She was scared, but she would not let fear get the best of her.

She grabbed hold of a rock for balance, pulled herself up and kept going.

When she reached a good spot she stopped to listen again. She heard car engines and indistinct voices, but she knew they probably came from the resort and downtown Cobalt rather than from anywhere close by. Sound carried across the lake. At night, in the quiet, you could often hear the sounds of people going about their lives in town. Right now they were doing their usual mundane things, while she was out here trying not to get killed. But at least she didn't hear Vincent closing in on her.

She continued on and finally the trees began to thin out. She was nearing the clearing around the Wilderness Photo Adventures office building.

If Vincent was waiting in the office, she was done for. If he was outside watching the clearing around the building, she would be an easy target. Her plan to come over here, break in and call the police suddenly seemed idiotic. But what else could she do? And now the icy rain was starting to fall heavily again.

She ran across the clearing to the back of the building and pressed up against it, waiting and listening. She hadn't heard any sound of Vincent in a while. Maybe he was a bad tracker and he'd gone in the wrong direction. Maybe he'd gotten lost in the woods. She almost smiled at the thought.

She crept to a corner where she could peek around the front of the building. She didn't see anybody. And there were no lights on inside the office other than the one she always left on in the lobby.

Her key was in her purse back in Vincent's truck, so she looked for something to break the front window. She figured it would be quicker and easier than the door, where the glass was much thicker. There were a couple of camp chairs on the patch of grass in front of the office and she grabbed one, swinging it toward the glass. It didn't break. She was cold and weak and barely able to hold on to the chair. She tried again, swinging it awkwardly but finally summoning up enough force to break the glass. She tried to think if she'd set the alarm before she'd left earlier, but couldn't remember. She hoped she'd set the alarm so the police would come to her rescue.

Right in front of her an office phone rested in the charger on Dottie's desk. She just needed something to cover the bottom of the windowsill so she could climb through it without cutting herself and bleeding to death before she could get help. She picked up the welcome mat from in front of the door, flung it over the windowsill and started to climb in. Someone grabbed the back of her neck.

"You *did* come up here." It was Vincent. And he was pointing a gun at her.

No. Caroline's heart sank. She had come so close. But she wasn't going to give up. She flailed her arms and then jammed her elbows backward, trying to hit him in the gut and knock the wind out of him.

It didn't work. Grunting and cursing, he yanked her away from the window and slapped his hand across her mouth. She kicked him and tried to trip him until finally he punched the side of her face. Her head snapped to the right and for a few seconds she felt a weird sensation like she wasn't quite connected to her body.

It took her a couple of minutes to realize

he was dragging her toward one of the storage sheds.

"No!" He shoved his hand over her mouth again before she could say anything else.

"Calm down, I'm not going to kill you yet. You'll still have time to do some of that praying you're so fond of," he sneered. "I'm just going to lock you up right now. One of my business partners will be by shortly to finish you off and dump you in the woods."

She struggled to get away from him and he gripped her more tightly.

"Don't you worry. I'll come up with some kind of story for the cops. Having a crashed truck and a shot-out window will make for a totally convincing story that there was an attack on the both of us. It doesn't even matter if they believe me. They can prove I shot a gun but there won't be any proof I killed you. I'll tell them I fired the shot from inside my truck in self-defense. Oh, and don't think breaking the window here will have the security company calling the cops for you. I came back in and turned off the alarm when we were all leaving for the day. You were so wrapped up in your boyfriend you didn't even notice."

Zane. Why hadn't she told him she loved him when she had the chance?

She tried again to trip Vincent and this time

he shoved the barrel of his gun into her ear. "I *will* kill you right here, right now, if you make me."

The blast of a gunshot tore through the night and suddenly Vincent was falling and pulling Caroline to the ground with him. Dark blood began soaking through his jacket near his shoulder and he groaned in pain.

Horrified and shaking, Caroline tried to push herself up off of him. Then she felt strong hands grab both her arms, untangle her from Vincent and set her on her feet.

Zane. He wrapped one strong arm around her while keeping his gun pointed at Vincent.

Vincent had dropped his gun and was rolling on the ground in pain. Zane kicked the gun away from his reach.

Cop cars come pouring up the drive, overshooting the parking lot and crossing the grass until they reached the spot where Vincent lay on the ground.

Matt got out of his patrol car, gun drawn, and moved toward them. "I got your message," he said to Zane without taking his eyes off Vincent. A second officer cuffed Vincent and called for an ambulance.

Zane tucked his gun into the back of his waistband and then wrapped his arms around

Caroline, holding her so close she could barely breathe. And that was just fine.

Both of them were soaking wet and cold. But together, they were warm.

"You found me," she whispered, starting to cry.

"I would never give up on you," he whispered back.

She blinked away her tears and leaned back so she could look at him. He was telling her the truth and she had no doubt about it. Even when she'd thought he'd given up on her all those years ago, he hadn't. He had been trying to protect her and her family.

And that past was firmly behind them. But what did the future hold?

She reached for both his hands and squeezed them. He gazed at her, and then slowly leaned forward to press his lips against hers. For the first time in a long while, everything felt all right. When the kiss ended, he looked at her with love and longing in his eyes.

Despite everything, she managed to grin at him. "Well, that took you long enough."

He tightened his arms around her and kissed her again. And he took his time.

SIXTEEN

Inside the Wilderness Photo Adventures office, Zane looked closely at Caroline. "Are you sure you're all right?"

He realized he'd already asked her that several times, but he needed to hear her reassurance again. Losing her had gripped him with a feeling of terror that was hard to shake. Even after he'd shot Vincent. And even after he'd held Caroline in his arms and kissed her. Twice. His heart had felt lifted up and filled with joy. But now it was weighted down again by concern. For Caroline, but also for himself.

"Your vital signs are good," the EMT said to Caroline, settling back in a chair and returning supplies to her medical bag. "You have no signs of frostbite. Your cuts and scrapes are cleaned up. You're warmed up and wearing dry clothes. Good thing some were handy." A slight smile crossed her lips as she glanced around the lobby. Caroline had been able to grab warm clothes from the shelves of her own business. "We can transport you to the hospital to get checked out if you like."

Caroline shook her head. "No, I just want to go home."

The EMT finished packing up and walked outside.

Vincent's gunshot wound was not fatal. He'd been transported to the hospital where he'd been met by detectives. According to Matt, he had offered a full confession and agreed to testify against the Seattle crime group he'd been aligned with, in return for reduced charges and a new identity. He'd already told them how to find his accomplice in town. The surviving gunman from the attack at the office complex had been arrested.

Zane grabbed a chair, placed it in front of Caroline and sat down. "When you said you wanted to go home, I'm hoping you meant go with me back to the ranch."

A tired smile slowly crossed her face. "That was exactly what I was thinking." Her smile slowly faded and Zane began to feel anxious. What if those kisses and that moment they'd just shared were all they would have? What if Caroline returned to keeping him at arm's length?

He couldn't imagine spending the rest of his

life without her. Or without the little boy who effortlessly had found a way into Zane's heart.

"The first thing I need to do is go see my mom and Dylan," Caroline continued. She sighed. "My poor mom. Once again I have to deliver bad news to her about an attack on me before she sees it on TV." She got to her feet and Zane stood, too.

"But you finally get to tell her some good news," Zane said. "The attacks on you are over. And she'll get some closure on why Owen was killed. It's still senseless, but at least some of her questions will finally be answered."

"That's true. And I guess if the police here and in Seattle can get things wrapped up and the bad guys behind all of this arrested pretty quickly, I won't have to worry about attracting danger to my mom and Dylan. I won't have to stay away from them any longer." She worried her bottom lip between her teeth for a moment. "The repairs to Owen's house aren't finished yet. I suppose I can stay at Rennie's, too, until we're able to move back in."

"Or you could bring them with you up to the ranch," Zane said hopefully. He dreaded the thought of them going their separate ways.

Caroline smiled. But then once again that

smile faded and her eyes teared up. "I don't think that's a good idea."

Zane's heart sank. He was going to lose her again. But then he already knew that, right? From the beginning they'd agreed they were working together for the sake of her safety and her family. And that after things went back to normal, they'd go their separate ways. No clinging to the past.

"We'll do whatever you want to do." He forced himself to say the right words, even though they stuck like glue in his mouth and it took everything he had to get them out.

He loved her. He probably always had. Even during those years when he thought he'd let her go. And love usually involved some kind of sacrifice. Sometimes it was something small, like apologizing even when you really didn't think you'd done anything wrong. Sometimes it was something big, like keeping your mouth shut about your own desires and letting someone walk away if that's what she wanted.

Tears started to roll down her cheeks and he put his arms around her. "You've been through a lot," he said. "Sometimes your emotions start to catch up with you once things quiet down. Come up to the ranch and bring your mom and Dylan anytime you want to. It's a very healing place. Living there has done a lot for me."

"No," she said, her voice muffled against his chest.

And then she shoved him away from her, hard. Her face was flushed and her eyes were fierce. "No!" She shook her head. "I can't keep doing this."

"All right," he said, having no idea what she was talking about. But she'd suffered so much. If an angry outburst would make her feel better, he could weather it.

"No, it's *not* all right." She turned away from him and started to pace. After a couple of turns she stopped in front of him and looked him in the eye. The tears had stopped. Her chin was lifted. She took a deep breath. "I can't keep doing this." She shook her head. "I can't be around you, living at the ranch with your family, knowing it's all going to end."

Zane's heart practically stopped beating. He was afraid to hope, but he let himself give in to the feeling, anyway. "What are you saying?" he asked softly.

"I'm saying I already fell in love with you once. After you came back into my life, I wanted to believe I was smart enough not to fall in love with you again." She shook her head, a quivering smile lifting the corners of her mouth. "I was wrong. And if you don't feel the same way, I can't hang around at your ranch and—"

"I love you, too." Zane reached out and pulled her to his chest, kissing her again and looking forward to many, many more kisses. She felt so right in his arms. A wave of relief swept through him. They were finally together. Back where they belonged.

Eight months later

Zane brushed his warm lips across Caroline's cheek, then she watched as he lifted her hand and pressed his lips to the golden wedding band he'd placed on her finger barely an hour ago. "Excuse me, Mrs. Coleman, but I'll get right back to you as soon as I can."

One more kiss, this one much more serious and lingering, reminded her that he'd promised to love, honor and cherish her for the rest of their lives. Then he winked at her and walked over to Dylan, letting the small boy lead him into the ranch house to retrieve the surprise Dylan had promised Caroline. She watched them walk together, both of them dressed alike in black Western-style suits, white shirts, black cowboy hats and narrow black ties.

Millie followed them, wagging her tail. She had taken well to being a ranch dog, with lots of other animals and people to play with. But she still liked to keep her eye on her boy.

Zane's dad hadn't attended the wedding. Zane had called the number Lee had given him and left a message, but got no response. So he'd left a paper invitation for him at the Bull Pine Tavern.

After that, Lee called Zane to say he wasn't coming. But the fact that he'd actually made the call was something. They would keep inviting him to family events. Maybe one day he would accept, and perhaps one day a very lost man would be called to faith. Stranger things had happened. Caroline had experienced that for herself. For several years she couldn't possibly have imagined a way she and Zane would ever get back together. Or that she would ever want to.

It was just past sunset on a summer evening. The grounds of the Rocking Star Ranch looked like a fairyland, with twinkling lights strung along the porch of the ranch house and wrapped among the smaller nearby trees. The ceremony had taken place outdoors just before sunset. The reception, still going strong, was set up in the barn. It was beautifully decorated, with the tables and chairs, along with the decorating expertise, lent by the resort.

Rowena Sauceda didn't hold a grudge against Caroline for believing Vincent's false accusation of her. And she wasn't the heartless person she was reputed to be. She was simply a strong businesswoman who always strived to get results. Unfortunately, that made some people bitter and jealous and prone to malicious gossip about her.

After acknowledging that Caroline would never sell the Wilderness Photo Adventures property to the resort, Rowena had extended an offer for the resort to work through Caroline's company, arranging special packages for the resort guests that helped both their businesses. So far things were going well. In an ironic turn of events, Vincent sold his ten percent share in the company to Caroline so he could get some quick cash to hire a defense attorney.

Michelle had suspended her bid for custody of Dylan after she was challenged by Caroline's lawyer. What sort of future Michelle would choose for herself remained to be seen.

Caroline's mother sauntered up beside her and wrapped an arm around her shoulder.

"Oh, honey, I know I've already said it but you look beautiful."

"Thank you, Mom."

"And you looked especially beautiful standing beside Zane."

"Oh, Mom."

Owen's house had been repaired and Caroline's mom had moved back into it. Jack and Rose had tried to get her to move up to the ranch with Caroline and Dylan, but she'd insisted she wanted to stay in the house and be closer to town for the time being.

Caroline visited her mom every weekday on her way to the Wilderness Photo Adventures office, and made sure her mom got lots of time to play with her grandson.

Mom was working out with a personal trainer a couple of days a week, doing everything she could to become as fit as possible. She also spent more time at church and helping with a couple of local charities. She'd told Caroline that it wasn't until the events of the last year that she had realized she'd let herself step out of the mainstream of life. But now she was determined to get back into the swing of life and live each day she had left to the fullest.

Music drifted out of the barn where the

live band still played. Several guests wandered around the grounds, enjoying the pleasant summer evening, many of them carrying plates of food and setting up impromptu picnics.

"Who would have thought this would ever happen?" Caroline said, gesturing toward her wedding gown and then toward the barn and the wedding reception. There was so much more in her heart, but she couldn't say it without choking up. "God is good," she finally said.

"He is," her mom said, reaching for Caroline's hand and squeezing it. "But, oh, what a year."

Caroline felt herself laughing and crying at the same time. Somehow she had survived it all. And even though at times she had thought it impossible, she was actually *happy* again.

The deep healing had begun. And now her family was here, safe and together.

Thank You, Lord.

Zane stepped out of the front door of the ranch house on to the wraparound porch, Dylan beside him. Together, they were carrying something square and covered in white paper. It was decorated with what looked like an entire roll of tangled gold ribbon.

"What are those two up to?" her mom asked, quirking an eyebrow.

"Dylan said he had a surprise gift for me." Caroline smiled. Whatever it was, she would love it.

Her two favorite guys headed toward her. Zane had to walk stooped over so that Dylan could help carry the package. Seeing his strong hands holding the mystery gift next to Dylan's little ones sent Caroline's heart beating faster.

"This is from me!" Dylan called out as they walked up to her.

"Can I hold it and help Caroline open it?" Zane asked.

Dylan nodded and let go. Then he excitedly clasped his hands together in front of his chest and rocked back and forth on his heels as he grinned at Caroline.

Zane held the package out toward Caroline. "What is it?" she asked Dylan.

"Open it!"

She reached for a bit of the paper and started to tear. Not surprisingly, the wrapping job wasn't so good and the paper and ribbon quickly slipped aside. It was a picture frame. And under the glass was a recent picture of Caroline, her mom, Dylan and Zane.

And stuck next to it was a picture of Owen, Dylan and Millie.

Caroline felt a quivering in the center of her chest. "Of course your dad will always be a part of our family," she said, losing the battle to keep her voice from shaking. "I love it. Thank you."

She bent down to hug her nephew and he hugged her back. Before she could kiss him he took off running, Millie barking and chasing after him.

"Let me set this up so other people can see it," Caroline's mom said, taking the picture and walking toward the barn.

And then it was just Caroline and Zane and the soft summer night.

"We should probably go back in and mingle with our guests," Caroline said.

"Yeah." Zane took both her hands in his. Neither of them moved. They just gazed into each other's eyes. Caroline felt like she was finally connected to a piece of herself that had been missing.

"I was crazy to think I could ever live without you," Zane finally said.

"Well, now you don't have to." She gave him a quick kiss on the nose and then starting pulling him toward the party going on in the barn. "I like this song. Let's go put a little bit of that crazy to good use."

Too many years had passed since they'd last danced together. It was time to fix that.

* * * * *

If you loved this story,
don't miss these
other heart-stopping romances
by Jenna Night:

LAST STAND RANCH
HIGH DESERT HIDEAWAY

Find these and other great reads at
www.LoveInspired.com

Dear Reader,

We can't get through life without making a few assumptions. But sometimes what we assume about a person isn't true. Or maybe it isn't true any longer. All of us have been in a situation where we'd appreciate forgiveness and another chance.

I hope you enjoyed reading about Caroline and Zane as they learned to let go of the past and give each other room to grow into the person each of them was meant to be. And that, of course, opened up the pathway to love.

One of the things I enjoy most about writing for Love Inspired Suspense is connecting with my readers. You can find me at my website, Jennanight.com, on my Jenna Night Facebook page, or you can follow me on Twitter, @Night_Jenna. My email address is Jenna@Jennanight.com. I'd love to hear from you.

Jenna Night

Get 4 FREE REWARDS!

We'll send you 2 FREE Books plus 2 FREE Mystery Gifts.

Love Inspired® Suspense books feature Christian characters facing challenges to their faith... and lives.

FREE Value Over $20

YES! Please send me 2 FREE Love Inspired® Suspense novels and my 2 FREE mystery gifts (gifts are worth about $10 retail). After receiving them, if I don't wish to receive any more books, I can return the shipping statement marked "cancel." If I don't cancel, I will receive 4 brand-new novels every month and be billed just $5.24 each for the regular-print edition or $5.74 each for the larger-print edition in the U.S., or $5.74 each for the regular-print edition or $6.24 each for the larger-print edition in Canada. That's a savings of at least 13% off the cover price. It's quite a bargain! Shipping and handling is just 50¢ per book in the U.S. and 75¢ per book in Canada*. I understand that accepting the 2 free books and gifts places me under no obligation to buy anything. I can always return a shipment and cancel at any time. The free books and gifts are mine to keep no matter what I decide.

Choose one: ☐ **Love Inspired® Suspense Regular-Print**
(153/353 IDN GMY5)

☐ **Love Inspired® Suspense Larger-Print**
(107/307 IDN GMY5)

Name (please print)

Address   Apt. #

City   State/Province   Zip/Postal Code

Mail to the **Reader Service:**
IN U.S.A.: P.O. Box 1341, Buffalo, NY 14240-8531
IN CANADA: P.O. Box 603, Fort Erie, Ontario L2A 5X3

Want to try two free books from another series! Call 1-800-873-8635 or visit www.ReaderService.com.

Get 4 FREE REWARDS!

We'll send you 2 FREE Books plus 2 FREE Mystery Gifts.

Bad Boy Rancher
Karen Rock

Love Songs and Lullabies
Amy Vastine

Harlequin® Heartwarming™ **Larger-Print** books feature traditional values of home, family, community and most of all—love.

FREE Value Over $20

HOME *on the* RANCH

HRCBPA18

READERSERVICE.COM

Manage your account online!

- Review your order history
- Manage your payments
- Update your address

> ### We've designed the Reader Service website just for you.

Enjoy all the features!

- Discover new series available to you, and read excerpts from any series.
- Respond to mailings and special monthly offers.
- Browse the Bonus Bucks catalog and online-only exculsives.
- Share your feedback.

Visit us at:

ReaderService.com